knight's
wyrd

knight's
wyrd

debra doyle
and
james d. macdonald

TOR ◆ ESSENTIALS

TOR PUBLISHING GROUP

NEW YORK

KNIGHT'S WYRD

Copyright © 1992 by Debra Doyle and James D. Macdonald

Introduction copyright © 2023 by Sherwood Smith

A Tor Book
Published by Tom Doherty Associates / Tor Publishing Group
120 Broadway
New York, NY 10271

www.tor-forge.com

Tor® is a registered trademark of Macmillan Publishing Group, LLC.

Library of Congress Cataloging-in-Publication Data

Names: Doyle, Debra, 1952–2020 author. | Macdonald, James, 1954– author.
Title: Knight's wyrd / Debra Doyle and James D. Macdonald.
Description: First Tor Essentials edition. | New York : Tor Essentials, 2023.
Identifiers: LCCN 2023010757 (print) | LCCN 2023010758 (ebook) |
    ISBN 9781250877703 (trade paperback) | ISBN 9781250881991 (ebook)
Subjects: CYAC: Fantasy. | Knights and knighthood—Fiction. | Middle
    Ages—Fiction. | LCGFT: Fantasy fiction. | Novels.
Classification: LCC PZ7.D7735 Kn 2023 (print) | LCC PZ7.D7735 (ebook) |
    DDC [Fic]—dc23
LC record available at https://lccn.loc.gov/2023010757
LC ebook record available at https://lccn.loc.gov/2023010758

Our books may be purchased in bulk for promotional, educational, or business
use. Please contact your local bookseller or the Macmillan Corporate and
Premium Sales Department at 1-800-221-7945, extension 5442, or by email at
MacmillanSpecialMarkets@macmillan.com.

First Tor Essentials Edition: 2023

Printed in the United States of America

0   9   8   7   6   5   4   3   2   1

introduction

by Sherwood Smith

After I discovered Rosemary Sutcliff in fourth grade, I looked for stories set in medieval times. As the years went by, I noticed that most books by modern writers tended to either feature characters who thought and spoke like twentieth-century people, despite being dressed in tunics and houppelandes as they scratched their lice and spat rotten teeth, or suffer from flat characters who spoke forsoothly as the story trudged under the weight of See How Much Research I Did.

There are two that I come back to for rereading: one is Barbara Leonie Picard's *One Is One,* and the other is this book in your hands, *Knight's Wyrd* by Debra Doyle and James D. Macdonald.

Both these books are relatively short and appear to be simple, linear tales following a young man who wants to become a knight. Both were first published for young adults, though I first read them, and continue to reread them, as an adult.

Debra Doyle and James Macdonald certainly have the chops. They met and married while heavily involved with the Society for Creative Anachronism. James had gone into the navy—his form of chivalric adventure—while Debra was in the process of completing a doctorate in Anglo-Saxon studies. After James finished his naval hitch, they returned to the United States, where they settled down to raise their four kids and collaborate on nearly thirty books.

They each brought complementary strengths to their collaboration. James, who became an EMT (still on those chivalric adventures), would during his downtime spin out cinematic plots that Debra then turned into prose.

I am not a medieval scholar. I never made it past grade-school-level Latin, but I did toil through some Middle High German greats like Hartmann von Aue and Wolfram von Eschenbach while focusing on German literature. It was hard going much the same way reading Chaucer is, but I found it worthwhile because of the glimpses of medieval life gleaned through these texts. When I visited museums to look at medieval manuscripts, my attention was drawn not only to the beauties of hand-decorated Biblical texts, but also to scribbled notes at the edges of the elaborate lettering, and the quick sketches in margins, hints of what entertained those young monks and nuns during their long days in the scriptorium.

It's those little details, evocations of medieval life, that I find resonating through this fast-paced tale, which begins with Will Odosson, a squire soon to be knighted, fighting a couple of thieves about to rob an old woman of her pig. It's a hard fight, one he barely wins. He comes out of it badly beat up. He still must keep vigil in church all night before his knighting ceremony, enduring discomfort as he tries to focus his mind on knightly virtues instead of thinking over that fight. In the wee hours, Master Finn, a local wizard, comes to him and relates a vision—Will's wyrd. Unfortunately, it sounds pretty dire.

"Wizard"?

So this is a fantasy? Yes—and no, which is one of the reasons why this book works so very well. We know there were no wizards in medieval Europe. At least not by name. This wizard, who is friends with the local priest, is a reminder that during medieval times, science and religion went hand in hand. Scholarly clerics delved deeply into mystical as well as physical sciences as they tried to comprehend the cosmos.

The concept of the wyrd was well known; the word is a noun formed from the Old English verb *weorþan,* meaning "to come to pass; to become." Visions were very much a part of medieval life and literature. Ditto the belief that trolls and wights and ogres and ghosts walked the world.

The next day, Will and his buddies among the squires set out to catch up with the tourney season, because that's what young knights did, if they were not under orders to fight or defend their lord's castle; another of the ways I appreciate this story is the way Doyle and Macdonald evoke the medieval mindset with respect to chivalry, which nowadays we might regard as ritualized violence. Chivalry was a way to try to put the brakes on violence in a time when there wasn't much of a safety net for ordinary people. Tourneys were martial skills contests, with rules; ransoms for the winners, paid by the losers; and perhaps a prize offered by the host of the tourney. They were also great shows for the locals, in a time when you made your own entertainment.

Will briefly meets Isobel, the young woman he is destined to marry according to their respective parents' wishes, only to discover that she has her own goals, which don't necessarily include marriage to him. But then she disappears, and Will joins the search to find her because he takes his vows seriously, and tries to be a good knight.

He encounters other knights sworn to Duke Anlac, who are motivated by the usual human enthusiasms: greed, lust, ambition, and of course there are what we'd call the adrenaline junkies who are there for the fun of bashing up each other's armor, in spite of not only the dangers on the field, but accidents like running into a tree branch that you can't see in your heavy helm, and breaking your neck. As happens to Will's first opponent, Sir Beorn.

The downsides of fighting in armor, the battle-trained horses, the camaraderie and rivalry of the knights are so vividly evoked. So far, this is a fun, fast-paced tale with a dash of sensory realism to ground it.

But then comes this moment when Will attends Mass with the other knights:

"Hello, Will Odosson," whispered the man kneeling to Will's left. "I'm happy to see you here with us."

Will kept his head bowed, but looked sidelong at the speaker and saw only a dark form muffled in a hooded cloak. Then the speaker's head turned, and Will saw inside the deep hood the face of Sir Beorn of Stanburh.

Before Will could speak, another whisper came, this time from Will's right. "Hello, Will Odosson. I also am happy to see you here."

Will turned his head. Another muffled figure knelt beside him at his right hand. This one, too, he recognized: Sir Ohtere, whose corpse lay waxy-pale before the altar where the old priest chanted the funeral prayers.

On my first read, this is where the hairs on the back of my neck rose. It wasn't so much the ghosts—we've met at least one before—it was the repetition, the liminality of the scene, that threw me back into my readings in that difficult old German.

Until that moment I'd assumed I could predict the trajectory of the novel, which would follow the form popular for readers today. And I was fine with that: Will would fight some bad guys, overcome the sinister wyrd, earn a title, marry the sensible Isobel—happy ending.

But when he sees that ghost to his left, and another to his

right, I realized I had no idea where this story was going. The repetition, the symbols with sets of threes, the forests, the stonework that evokes the upward-reaching Gothic lines, resonate with all those ancient poems that were the huge bestsellers of the twelfth century.

The more I read, the stronger I felt that Doyle and Macdonald got as close to what delighted our medieval ancestors as a contemporary person can, giving us a tale that might have been shared on snowy winters' evenings during the time when jousting and tourneys were still being fought. Questions of honor and meaning, friendship and enmity, horror and awe, and of course laughter, entertained people a millennium ago, as they do now. *Knight's Wyrd* shimmers with emotional complexity and liminal engagement with the numinous, evoking the mindset of a thousand years ago in a way that I find essential for a medieval story.

for professor russell peck—

"a wight of mickle lore."

authors' note

Anglia isn't England, in spite of the occasional similarities, and the background of *Knight's Wyrd* isn't meant to reflect English history in the world as we know it. Among the more obvious differences: in the real world, the Giants' Causeway between Great Britain and Ireland is a natural stone formation (and mostly submerged, at that); and the island of Britain has never been inhabited by giants, ogres, unicorns, or other magical beasts.

A few words on pronunciation may be helpful as well. Most of the names are pronounced as they appear but with vowel sounds more like those of modern French or German. The letter *h* in words like *Ohtere* and *Stanburh* represents a breathy, back-of-the-throat *kh*-sound like the *ch* in the Scots *loch*. *Ohtere* is pronounced in three syllables, as *Okh-ter-uh; Seamus* as *Shaymus;* and *Raeda* in two syllables with the *ae* sounding like the *a* in *hat*. *Wyrd* is pronounced with a vowel sound somewhere between *word* and *weird;* and *Gyfre* and *ogre,* in spite of their spellings, are pronounced *Gyf-fer* and *oh-grr*.

knight's
wyrd

chapter
1

The spring rain had fallen for a week on Restonbury Castle, but on the day before Will Odosson's knighting the clouds parted and the sun came out to dry the steaming earth. Squires and bachelor knights poured out of the castle like wild ponies escaping through a broken gate, to work off their excess energy in hunting the Baron of Restonbury's deer.

Will felt glad to ride out of the castle for a few hours. Knighthood was a solemn calling, and all during the long and rainy week Father Padraic the priest, and Master Finn the baron's wizard, had taken the opportunity to put the finishing touches on years of lectures.

"If it wasn't one of them, it was the other," he said to his friend and fellow squire Tostig Raeda, the redheaded son of Restonbury's shire-reeve. "I've heard enough about the mysteries of knighthood over the past seven days to last me the rest of my life."

"They just want to make sure you don't disgrace the barony when you ride out to the tourneys," Tostig replied. "Nothing mysterious about that."

"Just you wait," put in Seamus of Ierne, another of the squires. He was a distant cousin of Will's on Will's mother's side, and the youngest son in a family that had been noble long before Duke Rollo sailed from Norroena to break Anglia in half. "Once Will gets his spurs, he'll be so full of mysteriousness the rest of us won't be able to talk to him."

Garth of Orwick—a Nordanglian, and at twenty-three the oldest of Baron Odo's household knights—regarded the squires with mock severity. "A good thing, too," he said. "Maybe we can get some work out of the rest of you for a change."

"Who do you think's been doing most of it all along?" Will asked. "Don't worry, though—you've still got Ranulf if you need something done."

As he spoke, Will glanced over at his younger brother, who was riding nearby. Ranulf looked both flattered and a little nervous—he was only twelve to Will's eighteen, and hadn't been a squire long enough to shed his awe of the knights with their white belts and gilded spurs and huge, thundering warhorses.

Will grinned. After his little brother had cleaned enough of the leather belts and polished enough of the spurs and rubbed down enough of the horses, he'd be looking at knighthood in a clearer light. Will opened his mouth to say as much, but before he could speak the hounds began to bay. Off in the woods the baron's chief huntsman blew his horn to begin driving the prey toward the waiting knights.

Moments later, Will heard crashing noises in the underbrush. A white deer burst out from among the leaves. Against the bright golden green of the early spring foliage, the pale shape of the running deer gleamed like a streak of silver. The hounds ran faster as their quarry came into view, while the troop of knights and squires increased their speed to match.

Will galloped along with the rest. His horse, Grey Gyfre, soon brought him up to the forefront of the riders, overtaking the knights on their heavier chargers. The wind of his passage blew his ginger-colored hair off his forehead and back past his ears.

The white deer was drawing ahead again. The belling of the pack grew loud and fierce. Will leaned forward over Gyfre's neck and strove to narrow the gap between himself and the plunging, panting deer. Somewhere behind him another knight shouted his name, and Tostig Raeda gave a high, piercing whistle. But the clamor of the hounds sounded even louder than the voices of his friends, and the drumming of Gyfre's hooves on the woodland turf seemed to roar in his ears like the sea.

Then, as suddenly as it had appeared, the white deer vanished. The voices of the pack fell silent. And Will saw that except for Grey Gyfre and a single lop-eared hound, he was alone in the forest.

He looked about for landmarks—some misshapen lump of rock or lightning-struck tree that might set this part of the forest off from all the others—and found nothing. He waited quietly for a few minutes, listening for the sound of the hunt in the distance. All he heard was his own slow, regular breathing, underlaid with the faint clink and squeak of Gyfre's saddle and bridle, and the whuffling noises made by the hound as it sniffed around the roots of the trees.

Will frowned. He wasn't afraid of the trolls and other unpleasant creatures who still infested the wilder parts of Suthanglia—not in broad daylight and this close to home, with a good horse under him and a sword by his side. But working his way back by the lie of the land and the angle of the sun was going to take time, and he didn't have a hope of slipping into the castle unnoticed. He was, after all, the lord of Restonbury's eldest son and heir, whose knighting tomorrow was the reason for all the celebration and overcrowding.

"Blast it," he told the hound. "I don't want to spend the rest of my life hearing about how I got lost in the woods the day before Duke Anlac made me a knight."

The hound lolled out its tongue and grinned at him.

"Learn to live with it, you say?" Will sighed. "You're probably right. Well, let's get started."

He stayed where he was for a moment or so longer, sorting out his memories of the chase. The forest lay to the north and west of Restonbury, and the hunting party had set out heading northward. But which way had the deer led them after that? He wasn't sure. After some thought, he decided to ride southward, in the hope of breaking free of the forest. Once out in the open, he could spot the grey stone towers of Restonbury Castle as soon as they thrust up over the horizon.

He squinted upward through the green leaves at the general position of the sun and started out toward what he hoped would be the south. He'd been riding for a few minutes in that direction when he heard a commotion in the underbrush ahead: hoarse shouts, a cracked voice shrieking, and the high-pitched squeal of an unhappy pig.

The noise was loud enough to mask the sound of his approach. The angry yells grew louder, the curses more bitter. Will urged his horse onward in the direction of the noise.

He rode out of the underbrush into a forest glade. A narrow footpath, half overgrown, came out of the woods to his left and ran across the open ground into the shadows of the trees on the other side. An old woman in drab homespun stood in the middle of the path, her hands clenched on one end of a stout rope. The other end of the rope was tied around the neck of a well-fleshed milk-white pig. Two large men with drawn swords circled around them both.

"Come on now, granny," one man said. The words were soft and wheedling, but the heavy blade in his right hand gave his voice the lie. "We don't want to hurt you. Just give us the piggie and go on your way."

As he spoke, the other man lunged for the pig. The plump

beast squirmed free with surprising agility. It gave a fierce squeal and dashed out of the outlaw's reach.

The woman wound the rope even tighter around her knobby, work-soiled hands. "He's mine, I tell you," she said, hauling the pig in close against her patched and mended skirt. "He's all that I have."

"He's too good an animal for the likes of you," said the man who had grabbed for the pig. "I'll wager you stole him from some lord's pigsty."

"I never did!" cried the old woman. "I bought him for tuppence at the market-fair in Delminster."

The other man seized her from behind as she spoke. "You should have saved your coppers, granny. He's ours now. Take the pig, Osbert."

Will reined in Gyfre to a stop and drew his sword. The blade left its sheath with a steely whisper. He moistened his lips with his tongue.

"Leave the woman alone."

The two outlaws turned at the sound of his voice. They looked from his bare sword to the horse he sat on—no knight's war-horse, as he was not yet a knight, but a trim, fast animal—and then back at him. The man who had been holding the old woman spoke first.

"Here, now, son. You wouldn't take advantage of us by using that beast, would you? Where's the honor in that? Dismount and fight us man to man."

Will looked at the two outlaws. Neither one was armored, and neither had a shield. Will wore his coat of mail and carried his shield slung on his back. Mounted, he held every advantage except that of numbers alone, and even at two against one the men on foot would be hard pressed.

"I'm not Baron Odo's executioner," he said. "Go away, and leave Restonbury in peace."

He held his breath, hoping that the outlaws would take the chance to escape without a fight. But the two men didn't run. Instead they looked at each other and lifted their swords.

The second outlaw looked back at Will and sneered. "Come on and ride us down, boy. Show how brave a lord on horseback can be against poor folk on foot."

Will felt the heat of anger rise in his cheeks. He swung down from the saddle onto the turf and slid his left arm through the straps of his shield.

"No," he said. "You asked for combat on foot, and you can have it."

The outlaws said nothing. The first man shifted his sword into a two-handed grip and took a step forward to Will's right. A few feet away, his fellow moved out toward Will's left.

Will saw the easy smoothness of the maneuver and felt his mouth go dry. Too late, he realized the truth: He wasn't facing untrained peasants driven to banditry by misfortune or the cruelties of a harsh overlord. These two had fought as a team for a long time. It showed in the steady pace of their advance, in how they moved in on him together while keeping out of each other's reach—and in the practiced way they'd goaded him into offering an uneven contest.

They'd played him for a fool, and now he was likely to die of it. He hoped the old woman had taken her pig and run off while she had the chance, so that some good, at least, would come of the fight; but he didn't dare glance away from the outlaws to see if she had gone.

The first man gave a yell and dashed at Will, swinging his sword as he ran. The sun made the steel into a blazing bar of light as it came down. Will watched it, fascinated—but no amount of fascination could take away what he'd practiced every day of his life since he first held a wooden sword in one childish hand. His shield came up to block the blow, and his sword swung round in a counter-strike.

The outlaw's sword crashed into the metal rim of Will's shield, and Will's left arm vibrated clear up to the shoulder with the force of the impact. The man was strong. Will's own sword continued its arc inward toward the outlaw's left side, but the other man twisted out of the way and the blade met nothing but air. Worse, the blow pulled Will out of line so that his shield was lowered and his right shoulder exposed.

Clumsy, he thought. *With moves like that I* deserve *to lose this fight.*

The outlaw laughed at him, saying, "We'll sell your horse in Delminster tomorrow, boy. Ride him down, Osbert!"

Then Will saw that the second man had gone over to Gyfre and leapt into the saddle. "Now who's the lord on horseback?" he shouted, and kicked the horse in the ribs with both heels.

But Gyfre had been well trained by Restonbury's master of horse and would not move for any rider but his own. He tossed his head at the outlaw's kicks and curses, and stood as if he'd taken root.

Will knew that this would be his last, best chance. He brought his shield up and shoved it toward the man in front of him. He struck again and again as he pushed forward, but the outlaw knocked aside each blow, and the return strokes came just as fast.

"Osbert!" the outlaw shouted. "Leave that horse and get over here!"

Will swung at the lower part of the outlaw's legs, and this time his luck held—the man brought his sword down into the way of the feint, leaving his side and upper thigh unprotected. Will swept his blade upward in a rising blow and felt a dull impact as the sharp edge bit into flesh. A red stain spread out over the dirty wool of the man's cross-gartered hose. He fell, grasping his wounded leg with both hands.

Before Will could recover, the second outlaw had jumped down from Gyfre's back and come to join the fight. Osbert gripped his sword one-handed; with his free hand, he grabbed the rim of Will's shield and pulled. Will pulled back, trying to bring his shield into line before Osbert could strike through the opening their tug-of-war had created.

Will was off balance, and Osbert had the strength of desperation in his arm. The battle might have been lost—except that something grey flashed into Will's field of vision, and the lop-eared hound leapt snarling onto the outlaw's back.

Osbert staggered and lost his grip on the rim of the shield. Once again Will's long hours of training let him go on without stopping to think. He thrust his blade out toward the other man's chest. The point met solid resistance, then pushed on forward, and the man went down.

Something heavy and hard struck Will across the backs of both legs, slamming his mail against his flesh and forcing him to his knees. The man he'd taken out earlier had swung at him from the ground, striking hard enough to hamstring him if his armor hadn't taken the blow.

The wounded outlaw laughed—a breathless, choking noise mixed with gasps of pain. Lunging forward again from where he lay, he drove in another blow with the strength of his arms and shoulders alone. Will rolled away and cut down with his sword. The man lay still.

Will pushed himself up onto his knees. His muscles trembled from the effort of the fight, and the blood rushed in his ears. The backs of his legs hurt where the sword had crashed into them. His armor had kept the blade from cutting into his flesh, but he'd have blue and purple bruises before nightfall just the same.

He shook his head to clear it and got to his feet. The lop-eared hound danced up to him, tail wagging. He slipped his left arm out of the shield straps and scratched the animal behind the ears.

"Good dog," he said. "If it weren't for you . . ."

He let the sentence trail off unfinished and looked about the sunlit glade. He'd nearly died here, through his own foolishness. If he'd stayed on horseback, the outlaws would never have had a chance. And if he'd just given his father's battle cry and charged at them full tilt, they probably would have broken and run away without even bothering to fight.

Now both men lay dead on the trampled grass, and he was alive, though he wasn't certain he deserved to be. A few yards away the old woman still stood, with the white pig on its length of rope pressing against her legs like a frightened puppy.

Will let out his breath. *All this,* he thought, *over a pig.*

chapter
2

Later that evening in the chapel at Restonbury, Will knelt before the altar and tried to think of something besides the soreness in his legs. This was his vigil, kept during the hours of darkness on the eve of his knighting. If he couldn't endure a little discomfort now, he didn't deserve the honor.

In the back of Will's mind, a skeptical voice pointed out that his father and Duke Anlac would go through with knighting him whether he thought himself worthy or not. Baron Odo's unswerving loyalty kept the King's Peace in this part of the country; and Duke Anlac, if he wanted to succeed his grandfather on the throne of Suthanglia, would need the same loyalty from Odo's son and heir. Therefore Anlac had come to knight William Odosson with his own hands, and take Will's oath of fealty before the crowd of noble guests.

Will shifted his weight from one knee to the other. Besides his bruises, the muscles in his calves and thighs still ached from the long walk home. He'd been lucky in one thing, at least: The old woman had known the way to Restonbury Town, and with her directions to guide him he'd managed to reach the castle before dark. But he'd had to go on foot the whole distance, with the bodies of the two outlaws slung across Grey Gyfre's back. The horse hadn't liked carrying that burden, and Will hadn't enjoyed the experience either, but not even bandits deserved to lie nameless and unburied in the deep woods.

These two might still go unburied—Duke Anlac believed in hanging up the bodies of criminals who broke the King's Law—but they wouldn't be nameless. Thurstan the Shire-reeve, the father of Tostig Raeda, had recognized both of them as soon as Will arrived at the castle.

"I'd heard there was a pair of wolfsheads about," he'd commented, "and these look like the fellows. Osbert of Orkney and Hywel de Galis. The yeomanry's been beating the bushes for them without much luck, this whole week past."

After that Will encountered none of the teasing he'd expected for getting separated from the hunting party. Instead he found himself something of a hero. But when he mentioned the white deer that had led him astray in the first place, the other hunters all shook their heads. Every deer taken that day had been of the normal reddish brown kind, and no one remembered chasing after a white deer at all.

"Is my memory that bad," Will murmured, "or did I dream it?" He flinched at the loudness of his voice in the quiet chapel and forced his attention back to the altar.

A sword lay there, its naked blade washed with yellow candle-glow. The sword was truth, Father Padraic had said during one of his many lectures, and its edges were honor and justice. Will knew that he should be thinking about those noble virtues, but his thoughts kept circling back to the fight in the woods. He'd almost died there, and two men were dead because of him—and if truth, honor, and justice had been anywhere about during that fight he hadn't noticed them at the time.

"Things are not always as they seem."

Will slewed his head and shoulders around to look at the speaker, a tall, lean-featured man in a dark robe, with the hood thrown back from a thinning shock of sandy hair.

"Master Finn," Will said in surprise. The wizard had been a part of life in Restonbury for as long as Will could remember, and Baron Odo valued his counsel, but the chapel had never been one of his favored retreats.

Nor had Finn ever been one to break in on someone else's private meditations. Will felt a stirring of unease. The knighting of a baron's heir was not supposed to bring a look of trouble to the eyes of the baron's most foresighted adviser.

"What do you mean, 'not always as they seem'?" he asked.

Finn raised one hand and pointed at the sword lying on the altar. "Consider that blade. What is it to you? Truth and honor and justice, as Father Padraic would have it? Or is it like the white belt and gilded spurs, or the chain of metal links—simply one of those things that mark a knight?"

"I don't know," Will said. "What *should* it be?"

"After what happened this afternoon," said Finn, "you ought to know the answer without being told. A blade has two edges, and a point besides—and both point and edge can kill."

"What do you mean?"

A distant expression came into the wizard's pale eyes. It was his look of prophecy, and Will felt the first touch of fear, like a cold finger on the back of his neck.

"You will find out soon enough," Finn said. "You won't ever be the lord of Restonbury or sit in your father's seat."

Will swallowed. "My brother—?"

The wizard nodded. "Yes. You can take up the sword and be Sir William Odosson all your life long—but you'll meet death before any other title comes to you."

For a long time Will said nothing. Then he sighed. "Ranulf's a good lad; he'll do well with the barony. Just the same . . . Master Finn, are you certain Restonbury goes to him?"

"It is your wyrd," said Finn. "I have seen it."

Wyrd . . . the shape of what would happen, the nature of

things as they had to be. Will drew a long, slow breath, let it out again, and drew another.

"Why?" he asked, and in spite of all the effort his voice cracked on the question, sounding high and frightened as it echoed off the vaulted ceiling. "I know that if you've seen it, then it must be true. But why did you have to tell me about it tonight?"

"Because you still have a life to live in the world," said the wizard. "Can you tell me what sort of life it will be?"

Will shook his head. "This morning, I could have. But not tonight."

"Then you have something to think about between now and sunrise," said Master Finn. "And I've been here long enough." The wizard smiled a little, rather sadly. "Our good Father Padraic, if he knew, would scold me for coming here at all, and for burdening you with too much knowledge."

Before Will could reply, the wizard turned and left the chapel, his black robe fading into the shadows. Will looked for a moment longer at the darkness where the wizard had gone, and then turned again to the altar.

The sword lay there as before, three feet of steel gleaming dully in the candlelight.

Will shivered. In his mind's eye, sharp and clear, was the memory of the outlaw's blade, catching fire in the sunlight as it came sweeping down toward his uncovered head. He'd stopped the blow in time, and it was his weapon, not the outlaw's, that had carried death. But it could have been him lying there on the bloodstained grass.

Would be him, someday, if he took the sword. Master Finn had seen it, and what the wizard saw was always true.

"What can I do?" he whispered. He gripped his hands together to stop their shaking. "Where can I go?"

No voice spoke out of the silent chapel to guide him, only the rustling echo of his own voice. *Go . . . go . . . go.*

He pressed his clasped hands against his mouth to keep himself from speaking any further. But the pictures ran on unchecked in his mind: himself turning away from the sword on the altar, slipping out unnoticed to the stables, saddling up Grey Gyfre, and taking to the road. The world was wide; he could leave Restonbury far behind, go to Nordanglia or Galis, Ierne or Caledon, and try to outrun his fate.

But—*"It is your wyrd,"* Finn had said. *"I have seen it."*

A strangled laugh, almost a sob, caught at Will's throat. He was no seer, and the pictures in his mind meant nothing. He could ride to the farthest shores of the kingdom, he could take ship for Thule or Hy-Brasil, he could live in a cave in the woods like a hermit—it was all one. In the end, his wyrd would take shape as it must. He would die, and Ranulf Odosson, younger son though he now was, would go on to become the Baron of Restonbury.

Will bit at the knuckles of his clasped hands and tasted blood. Now he understood what the wizard had meant about living in the world. The choice was a bitter one. He could run, to the everlasting shame of his father's name and his own, and play hide-and-seek with death for as long as possible before the end. Or he could stay here, take his vows of knighthood, give Duke Anlac his oath of fealty, and let the wyrd Finn had seen for him come however it would.

"What's the answer?" he muttered against his clasped hands. "What do I do? Somebody please tell me—*what do I do?*"

At sunrise Father Padraic and Master Finn came for him together. He went with them unprotesting, moving slowly on legs grown stiff from kneeling all night before the altar.

His mind felt as numb as the rest of him. All through the

hours of his vigil, he'd struggled with the wizard's prophecy—
one moment close to leaping up and fleeing headlong, the next
instant determined to stay. Morning found him exhausted
and still uncertain of what he was going to do. He let the priest
and the wizard lead him from the chapel and escort him to
the small room near the great hall where his feast-day clothing
awaited him.

Yesterday evening, before his vigil, he had bathed and
changed his rough wool tunic for one of clean linen. Now Father Padraic held out to him a long, full-sleeved overtunic of
soft velvet in the blue and gold that were Baron Odo's colors. It
was a fine garment for the knighting of Restonbury's heir, and
Will flinched in spite of himself at the sight of it.

The priest looked startled. "Here, now—what's wrong?"

"Nothing," muttered Will. Beyond Padraic, in the doorway,
he saw Master Finn gazing at him with something like pity in
his pale grey eyes.

Quickly, almost angrily, Will took the tunic and pulled it
over his head. The soft fabric seemed to fall onto his shoulders
with a weight heavier than any coat of mail. He shivered, and
forced himself to stand still while the priest and the wizard
draped a cloak of blue wool around him and fastened it with a
golden pin.

When he was dressed, Finn and Padraic led him out of the
robing room and up to the doors of the hall. He stepped over
the threshold and came to a halt.

Will had lived all his life in Restonbury Castle, but never before had he seen the great hall in such a state of glory as this.
Decorations had gone up during the hours he'd kept vigil in
the chapel, and the banners of the noble guests made a blaze of
color against the stone walls and wooden roofbeams. Under the
banners, the long, high-ceilinged room was packed with on-
lookers. Some of them Will had known all his life—his mother

and sister and brother, his fellow squires, his father's household knights—but others he had never seen before. Those would be members of Duke Anlac's court, come here with their lord to do Will honor at his knighting.

The duke himself sat in the High Seat at the end of the great hall, and Baron Odo sat at the duke's right hand. A sheathed sword lay across the baron's lap. Both men seemed very far away from where Will stood. For a moment he wanted to turn and run, but the memory of Finn's pitying glance held him fixed in place.

At the same time, he hesitated to go forward. Then Master Finn coughed, and Father Padraic gave his arm a gentle tug. Half involuntarily, Will allowed the priest and the wizard to lead him down the length of the hall between the ranks of witnesses, until he stood in front of Duke Anlac.

"Kneel," the duke commanded.

Will knelt. The rushes spread on the floor of the hall made it warmer than the chapel floor had been, and a bit easier on the knees, but the sword that lay sheathed across his father's lap was the same one that had lain all night on the chapel altar. He wanted to look away, but he knew that he could not. If he faltered now, he would shame Baron Odo in his own hall and in the presence of his lord the duke.

No matter what happens to me afterward, Will thought, *I can't do that to him.*

Baron Odo lifted up the sword and gave it to Anlac. The duke stood and unsheathed the blade. Point and edge glittered in the morning sunlight slanting down through the high clerestory windows of the great hall.

Duke Anlac was a powerful man, with grey streaking the black of his beard. His hair curled forward across his forehead, and his eyes glittered like the sword as he spoke.

"Who comes before me?"

Will ran his tongue over lips gone suddenly dry. He couldn't run now—it was too late for that. All he could do was make the responses Finn and Padraic had taught him.

"I am William Odosson of Restonbury, my lord."

"And what do you ask?"

Will's voice was faint, but he managed to keep it steady. "I ask to be knighted, my lord."

Duke Anlac laid the naked sword on William's left shoulder, letting him feel the weight of it. "You are aware," the duke said, "that if I should cut off your head here and now, no man could say I did wrong? For no one deserves knighting, and to ask to be knighted is to presume worth that you do not have."

The stern words had more truth to them than Duke Anlac knew, Will thought. *What would he do if I told him I almost wasn't here to come forward at all? That I only stayed because I was too much of a coward to run away?*

"Yes, my lord," he whispered. "I know."

Duke Anlac raised his arm, and swung the sword full at Will's unprotected neck. Will didn't move. Both Finn and Padraic had warned him of this many times in the past week—reminding him that if he flinched, and the duke misjudged, then he might die without being knighted at all.

But Anlac pulled the blow so that it stopped short a fraction of an inch from the flesh. Instead of striking home, he tapped the cold edge lightly against Will's neck, first on the left side, then on the right.

"I dub you knight," he said. "Take these blows and no others. Keep the faith, uphold justice, and protect the innocent. Now rise, Sir William Odosson of Restonbury, and swear your fealty."

Will felt lightheaded, as if all his movements were actions in a dream. Any moment now, he thought, he would wake up and find out he'd dozed off while kneeling on the chapel floor.

Still half-dazed, he got to his feet and extended his hands before him, palm to palm.

Duke Anlac took Will's hands between his own.

"When you were a squire," the duke said, "you could not swear, for your word was nothing. Now that you are a knight, your word is all you are. Are you my man?"

Will drew a deep breath. This time his voice was loud enough to carry beyond himself and the duke. "I am."

"Very well." The duke gestured, and Finn and Padraic came forward. They buckled William's white swordbelt to him, the sheath hanging empty at his left side. They fastened on his golden spurs and put the silver chain around his neck.

"Let all who see be witness," Duke Anlac said, "that Sir William Odosson of Restonbury is a knight, and is my man."

With that he reversed the sword and held it out toward Will, pommel foremost.

One last time Will hesitated. If Master Finn spoke true—and he had never known the wizard to tell a lie—it was his own death the duke was giving him.

But he had not run in the hours of darkness, and now he was a knight and the duke's sworn man. He reached out and closed his hand around the grip of the sword.

"Long live Sir William!" shouted Will's brother Ranulf, his young voice cracking on the name.

As if that were a signal, the other witnesses raised such a cheer that the hall itself shook with the noise. Then Will realized that it wasn't the walls and floor that were shaking, but his own hand on the grip of the sword. Carefully, so no one would see him trembling, he sheathed the weapon and let himself be embraced first by the duke and then by his father.

After that, it seemed everybody in the hall came up to him at once, to hug him or slap him on the back or just squeeze his hand in a friendly grip. Courtesy demanded that he exchange cheerful greetings with them all. Somehow he managed to do so, but he was glad when the servers came in to set up the benches and the trestle tables for the feast. His legs ached from the long hours spent kneeling, and he thought that if he didn't get a chance to sit down soon, he would drop.

At the feast, Duke Anlac sat in the place of honor. Will, as the new-made knight, sat at his right hand, and the squires who served at the high table brought them the choicest portions of all the dishes. Will ate some of everything—his mother, who had planned the feast, would be distressed if he didn't, and the castle cook would be insulted as well—but the roast pork and stewed cabbage, the cinnamon wafers and the apples poached in wine, all were lacking their accustomed savor.

He chewed and swallowed, sipped sparingly at the goblet that stood by his plate, and gave polite replies to the questions Duke Anlac directed at him from time to time. But he felt light and detached, like a spider's web come loose from its moorings and floating on the wind, and neither questions nor answers stayed in his mind for long.

Gradually he became aware that he had been talking for several minutes, not to Duke Anlac, but to the thickset, bearded man on his own right. Somewhat to his dismay, he could not recall who the man was or what they had been talking about, but he saw that Duke Anlac appeared pleased by the conversation. With an effort, Will collected his wandering thoughts and concentrated them on his neighbor.

"Your father and I agree," the man was saying. "When you were a squire, the journey was too far, but now that you've been knighted it's high time you came north and paid us a visit."

"High time," echoed Will blankly. For a moment he didn't know what to say next. Then the courteous responses he'd learned by rote in boyhood came to his aid, and he added, "I'm honored by the invitation."

Now, if he could just remember who the bearded man was, and why Baron Odo thought he deserved visiting . . . but Will's neighbor was already smiling and shaking his head.

"It's all of us at Harrowholt who'll be honored," he said. "My girl Isobel especially. She's wanted to meet you for a long time now—wants to see what you look like, get to know you a little bit before the wedding, that sort of thing. Nearly broke her heart when I said the roads were too dangerous for her to travel south with me."

"Much too dangerous," agreed Will. He smiled back at the man and hoped that his own feelings didn't show so easily on

his face. He should have remembered Lady Isobel of Harrowholt and her father as well—Henry, that was the bearded man's
name, Baron Henry of Harrowholt. After all, the man was going to be his father-in-law someday.

Until now he'd never given much thought to the marriage
his father and Baron Henry had arranged years ago, when Lady
Isobel had been scarcely three years old and Will a few months
older. Like being knighted, and like becoming lord of Restonbury, the marriage had been something that would happen to
him some day in the future, and that didn't particularly need
attending to in the meantime. But Master Finn's warning had
changed all that: How could he wed Baron Henry's daughter
when his own life was bound for an early end?

I can't marry her, Will thought. If only Finn had prophesied
otherwise—but no, he'd seen the barony going to Will's brother
Ranulf. Without a child of her own to be Will's heir, Lady Isobel
would be just another young widow, and that was no life to wish
on a girl he'd never even met.

But the whole world loves a scandal, he thought. *If I back out
now, the gossip is certain to put all the blame on her.*

Will couldn't make up his mind which fate she'd think was
worse, being a widow or being an abandoned bride. All he
could see was that he was likely to hurt Isobel of Harrowholt
grievously no matter what he did.

Delay, he concluded. He'd have to hold off the match as long
as he could, until he found some way to free Lady Isobel from
the contract without dishonor, or—more probably—until Master Finn's vision came true and released her with his death.
Meanwhile, he was going to have to make that visit.

"Midsummer," he heard himself saying. It seemed he'd been
making polite conversation while his mind struggled with the
problem—he wondered what else he'd told the baron. "I'll be riding out to the tourneys as soon as the celebrations here are over,

and the tournament and fair at Saint Edwiga's fall on Midsummer Eve. That's close enough to Harrowholt to travel on afterward in your direction."

Baron Henry looked pleased. Talk at the high table turned to other matters, such as which one of the Old King's many grandchildren would have the best claim on Suthanglia when the kingdom's ancient monarch finally died, and whether the best falcons came from Galis or from the mountains of Caledon. Will took little part in the discussion, though he talked enough not to make his silence seem like rudeness. When Duke Anlac at last rose and took his leave, Will rose also.

He made his way through the crowded hall and headed for the door that led to the castle courtyard. The warm air inside the hall was thick with the mingled smells of food and close-packed humanity. Maybe the colder air outside would clear his head.

The courtyard was empty. Light spilled out from the doors of the hall and made the shadows look even darker. A damp, chilly wind, heavy with the promise of rain and muddy travel to come, blew across the stones. Shivering a little in spite of his cloak and his velvet tunic, Will continued down the steps of the hall and across the courtyard.

The squires and the bachelor knights who lived in the castle had quarters to themselves, separated from the main structure by a heavy stone wall. The first Baron of Restonbury, Will's great-grandfather, had taken no chances on letting ambitious young men sleep where they could attack him by surprise or open the gates to his enemies. Will had shared those quarters while he was a squire, and would keep on sharing them until he left home for the tournaments. After that, when he came back, his mother would insist on putting him in one of the tower rooms like any other guest.

If I come back, he thought. The wind struck him for a moment

with an even greater chill. Tourneys were mock combat, not
the real thing—but the weapons were real, and sometimes accidents happened.

He sighed. The knowledge of his fate changed nothing. He
would still leave Restonbury as he and his father had planned, to
avoid the troubles that sometimes occurred when a barony had
both a strong young heir and a lord still in the prime of life. Only
if danger threatened Restonbury itself would Will come home to
stay, because he might be needed to take his father's place.

But that would never happen; Master Finn had told him so. If
Will ever came back to Restonbury, it would be as a visitor—or
as a corpse.

He shook his head. Thoughts like that were what he'd left
the great hall to avoid. *You need to find some cheerful company,*
he told himself, and went on across the courtyard and through
the inner gate to the bachelors' quarters.

Most of the squires and the household knights had gotten
there before him, since they hadn't had to smile and nod and
say polite nothings to a dozen or so honored guests on their way
out. There was a good fire going in the small hearth, and from
the sound and smell of things, a livelier party than the one in
the great hall had already started.

The hubbub died as Will came in. Garth of Orwick looked
up from the pan of sausages he was frying at the edge of the
coals.

"Well, now," he said, "it's the new Sir William." He moved
the sausages away from the coals and stood up. "Are you ready
to learn the rest of the mysteries of knighthood?"

Will blinked. "More than I've learned already?"

"Oh, many more." Garth grinned and waved a hand at the
younger men and boys. "All you squires clear out of here. Come
back tomorrow."

Will thought he heard someone snicker. He looked at Garth

dubiously as the squires began heading for the door. "What sort of mysteries?"

"Mysterious ones," Garth assured him. "Very mysterious."

Will didn't find that much of an answer and opened his mouth to say so. The reply never emerged. Instead a cascade of cold water came out of nowhere and poured over his head. He spluttered for breath and turned to see two of the squires he'd thought were going outside. They carried an empty washtub that had—obviously—been full a moment earlier.

Garth was laughing as he gestured at the squires to come back in. "*That* is the biggest secret of knighthood," he told Will. "You might as well learn right now that being a knight doesn't mean you can walk in the rain without getting wet."

Now Will was laughing too, in spite of the water dripping off his hair and his sodden clothing, and the knights and squires were cheering him again.

"Put on something dry before we decide to throw you into the moat," said Garth. "The nobles up in the hall have had their celebration. This one is ours."

Tostig Raeda, who had taken Will's place as the senior squire, opened one of the clothes chests and brought out a new tunic. Will stripped out of his soggy finery right in the middle of the small hall and put on the dry linen. Then he shook his head, sending drops of water everywhere.

"I'm up for whatever you are," he said, taking the goblet that one of the junior squires passed to him. "Is anyone going to the tourney out at Strickland?"

"I am," said Garth. "Good fighting, and big ransoms for the winners—a poor bachelor knight can't afford to miss an occasion like that."

"I'll be coming with you," Will said. "My father won't like me staying around here with nothing to do. He'll think I'm just waiting for him to die so I can put on the title."

"Can't have people believing that," agreed Garth. "If you trust me not to lead you off north into the hands of my kinsmen, you can travel with me as long as you like."

Will sat down on one of the low footstools by the hearth and stretched out his legs toward the fire.

"I'm not important enough to bother leading off," he said, and took a drink from his goblet. "With the Old King marrying off his children and grandchildren and great-grandchildren on both sides of the border all these years, everybody with any ambition is already a member of the family. The son of a minor baron isn't going to make a difference to anyone."

"True enough," Garth agreed. "If there's such a thing as providing the kingdom with too many heirs, your king has certainly done it."

The older knight speared one of the sausages with his knife. Hot fat spurted out and sizzled on the cast-iron pan.

"Let me tell you," he went on between bites, "it's played hob with Nordanglia, too. I'll name no names, but we've got people who ought to be staying home and ruling their own lands playing politics down here instead."

"Can you blame them?" asked Seamus. "The crown of all Anglia is prize enough to tempt anyone."

"Not me," said Will, draining his goblet. "Politics puts me to sleep. Let's get on with the serious merrymaking."

Tostig refilled the goblet. Garth shoved one of the hot sausages in Will's direction with the tip of his knife. Seamus pulled a set of smallpipes out from under his cot and started playing a raucous tune.

Some time later, the party was still going on. Garth was in the middle of a complicated tale about a plowboy, an old woman, and the Bishop of Orwick's donkey when a knock sounded at the door. It was a page, a boy of about eleven, wearing Duke Anlac's colors.

"Sir William Odosson?"

Will unfolded himself from the stool by the fire and stood up. "Here I am."

The page bowed low. "My lord the duke wishes to speak with you outside."

"I'm at his service," said Will, bowing back. "Lead on."

The page escorted him out into the darkened courtyard. Duke Anlac was waiting, a heavy wool cloak wrapped about him against the night air. Will, cloakless in his borrowed tunic, shivered as the cold wind struck him. He went down on one knee to the duke, and saw as he rose that Anlac was gesturing the page away.

The secrecy disturbed Will a little. What kind of talk between lord and man needed to take place in a deserted corner at midnight? On the other hand, he reminded himself, it was the duke's right to summon and dismiss his servants as he chose.

"How may I serve you, my lord?" Will asked when the page had gone.

"It's a small matter," said the duke. "Perhaps no matter at all."

If that was so, Will wondered, then why couldn't it be openly spoken of—if not at the feast, then in the bachelors' hall afterward? But it wasn't his place to question the duke. He held his peace and waited for Anlac to go on.

"You ride to the northern marches this summer," said the duke. "Or so I heard you tell Henry of Harrowholt."

"That's true," Will said. "My father's given me leave to follow the tourneys."

"Excellent," said the duke. "You can be my eyes and ears on the border at the same time. The north country isn't rich, but the castles there are strong, and they command the roads from Nordanglia and Galis. Any man of mine who holds one must be loyal—otherwise he could make his fiefdom into a dagger for my back." Anlac paused. "Some of my northern vassals, I fear, are perhaps not as loyal as they should be."

"I don't even know most of them, my lord," said Will. "I can't help you there."

"That's where you're wrong. A stranger can see clearly what a friend might hide or an enemy might paint darker than truth would allow."

Will's lips tightened. "Are you asking me to be your spy, my lord?"

"No, no," said the duke. "You're my sworn man, and the son of my friend—I wouldn't press you into dishonorable service. I'm not asking you to find out any secret or hidden thing. Just tell me how things stand in the marches."

Will nodded slowly. "I'll do that, my lord."

"Very well." The duke turned to go.

"One thing more, Your Grace," Will said.

The duke turned.

"What if I should discover that some baron is not loyal?"

For a moment there was silence. Then the duke said, "*You* are loyal," and left without another word.

Will stood there staring at the duke's retreating back and tried to make sense of Anlac's last statement. Had Anlac been giving him an order, he wondered, or making him a promise?

"Maybe this is how I get killed," he muttered to himself. "Caught between a duke and his barons like a walnut in between two stones. No matter which rock hits the other, the walnut is the one that breaks."

chapter
4

A gust of wind whistled down across the courtyard, reminding Will that he'd left the knights' quarters wearing only a borrowed tunic. He headed back into the lesser hall, where the party was still going on. Seamus had put away the smallpipes and taken down the battered old harp that had hung on the wall as long as Will could remember. The Iernish squire had managed to bring the instrument into tune, and was striking the notes to "Duke Rollo's Wedding" while everybody else sang the verses.

Garth looked up from stirring a pot of spiced wine. "There you are," he said. "We thought you'd forgotten all about us. What did the duke want with Restonbury's newest knight?"

Will shrugged. "Nothing of any great importance," he said. "Just . . . talk."

Garth accepted the vague explanation without comment. He ladled spiced wine into a cup and held it out to Will. "Here—you look like you're half frozen, and you're shaking like you just saw a ghost." He paused and looked at Will more closely. "You didn't, did you?"

Will shook his head. "No ghost," he said. "I've never had the privilege of meeting one, in fact."

Seamus laid aside the harp and came forward for a cup

of wine. "I saw a ghost once," said the squire. "Back home in Kilmacduagh. A cousin of mine."

"What did it—he—look like?" Will asked.

"Just like he always did," said Seamus. "He showed up in the hall after dinner one night, and told the family not to expect him home from the fair, because he'd been eaten by an ogre on the road."

Garth filled a cup and handed it to Seamus. "Well, had he been?"

Seamus nodded. "One of our shepherds found the bones a few days later." The squire took a large gulp of the spiced wine and was silent for a moment. His freckled, snub-nosed face was somber as he continued, "We recognized them from a cloak-pin my cousin used to wear. There wasn't much else left to go by."

"Ogres are like that," agreed Garth. "Worse than wolves, they are—just one ogre turned man-eater can lay waste a whole village, people and livestock both."

"They can talk," Seamus said. "That's the worst part."

Tostig looked skeptical. His father, Thurstan, was a prosperous villager of the old Anglian stock, whose duties as the shire-reeve had never taken him any farther away from home than Duke Anlac's court at Delminster. For both father and son, anything that couldn't be found within the borders of Restonbury was probably nothing more than a fable. "Vermin like that? Tell us another one while you're at it."

"It's true," Seamus insisted. "The ogre that killed my cousin spoke Iernish as well as any mortal man, after my father and his brothers found it and brought it in to the hill-fort at Kilmacduagh. I heard it talking myself."

"That's different," conceded Tostig, "if you heard it. What did it say?"

"It laughed at us," Seamus said, "and called us names—'hairless weaklings' is the one I remember best. Then it broke the first set of chains our blacksmith put on it, and killed another man before my father and uncles managed to fetch new chains and bind it a second time."

"So what did you finally do with it?" asked Will.

"Our wizard tried every spell that he knew," Seamus said. "None of them could touch it. So my father sent to the High King at Tara and asked for the loan of his headsman."

"Your father cut off the ogre's head?"

"Well, actually, the headsman did it," Seamus said. "And then we burned the pieces."

"Good idea," said Garth. "My grandfather told me about an ogre up in Caledon whose body crawled about for three days looking for its missing head."

"I've heard that tale," put in Tostig Raeda. "The ogre found the head preserved in a wine barrel, set it on its shoulders, and went back home roaring drunk. Only *my* grandfather said it happened in Galis, not in Caledon."

They all laughed.

"Laugh if you like," said Garth, "but it's a dangerous world, my friends." Then he looked over at Will and grinned. "And as soon as Duke Anlac and his people go back home to Delminster, we're going out there to be dangerous in it."

A week later the two knights departed from Restonbury for the tourney at Strickland. Will rode on Grey Gyfre because he wanted the palfrey's endurance and even gait on the long road ahead, and Garth had chosen a similar mount. The squires Seamus and Tostig rode their own steeds behind, leading the packhorses and the tall, heavily muscled chargers.

The early morning air was still cold when they left the castle through the small door beside the gatehouse. The road to Strickland wound away northward, and they followed it through open country all morning. Just before noon they entered the deep woods.

"Do you suppose there's any wild boar hereabouts?" asked Garth as they rode under the trees. "A bit of roast pig would make good eating tonight."

"The last boar anyone saw in these woods," said Tostig Raeda, "turned out to be a female with all her piglets."

Will laughed. He remembered that occasion. "It was before you came to Restonbury," he told Garth. "But there were knights enough in the field that day—all of them climbing the trees to get away from her, and hanging on to the branches like armored fruit."

Garth snorted. "Where were you?"

"Climbing even higher than the knights," Will admitted. "I wasn't wearing as much iron, so I could move faster."

"Nothing dishonorable in that," said Garth. "What sort of knight wants minstrels to sing of how he died when the old sow and her litter cut him up and trampled him underfoot?"

They pressed on. The woods thinned out, and Will and his friends rode through open country for three days before coming to another forest. The road here hadn't been kept up as well as the roads in the south; it wasn't much more than a narrow track marked by thinner underbrush and thicker mud.

"We're coming up to the Giants' Bridge," Garth said at noon. "It's the best way to cross the Samsach River at this time of year."

"Are there really giants in the north country?" asked Tostig

Raeda. This journey to Strickland marked his first venture outside the borders of Restonbury. "Or is that just another story
people tell?"

Garth shrugged. "My grandfather used to say there were
still a few giants living up in the high mountains," he said. "I've
never seen one, mind you—but if there never were any giants,
then where did their walls and roads and bridges come from? I
have seen those."

Will glanced about, taking in the mud and uncleared brush
that blurred any distinction between road and forest. "This
can't be a giants' road we're on now."

It was Seamus who answered. "No. The giants' roads are
made of stone, like everything else they built. I've seen the biggest one—it runs like a great causeway between Ierne and Caledon, but the giants must have made it a long time ago. The sea
has risen since then, and at high tide the whole road is covered
by water."

Will tried to imagine a stone road stretching out into the sea,
and failed. "Is that how you came over from Ierne?"

Seamus shook his head. "Not me. It takes good luck and a
fast horse to make the crossing before the tide changes, and the
current is swift there. I took a boat from the Mull."

A little later the four travelers heard
the babble of fast water running over jumbled rocks. "That's the
Samsach, if I'm not mistaken," said Garth. "We're making good
time."

"And listen to the noise of it," said Seamus. "It'll be flooded
with the spring runoff from the snows in the western highlands.
I hope your bridge is still there—I don't fancy the thought of
fording a river in spate."

The bridge, when it came into view, looked solid enough to

withstand whole centuries of spring floods. The long-ago build-
ers had made it all of stone, cunningly fitting its huge blocks so
that the curve of the rounded arch remained strong and clean
beneath the overgrowth of moss and lichen.

Will looked at the massive structure—broad enough from
side to side for two loaded hay-wagons to pass each other without touching. "Giants, you say."

"Giants," Garth replied. "We should be grateful to them that
we don't all have to go wading."

They urged their horses forward onto the span, with Garth
in the lead. What came next happened almost too fast for Will's
eye to follow: Something long and brown came snaking up
from below to grasp the foreleg of Garth's steed, pulling horse
and rider together toward the side of the bridge.

The animal screamed in pain and terror—trying to rear up,
and failing. Its leg broke with a snapping sound, and the horse
fell, throwing Garth to the pavement. The horse vanished over
the side of the bridge; the other horses, panicking, raced on across
to the farther bank before their riders could bring them to a halt.

Will looked at the bridge. Garth lay on the stones with blood
running from his nose. Without thinking, Will swung down
from his saddle and ran back to kneel by Garth's side. He had
his sword bare in his hand, although he couldn't remember
drawing it—everything had happened too fast.

"Garth, get up!"

Garth was already trying to rise. He'd been lucky in his fall,
getting the wind knocked out of him but nothing worse. Still
gripping his sword, Will used his left arm to pull Garth onto
his feet. Then he helped him stumble forward off the bridge.
They didn't stop until they reached the shore.

The squires were waiting for them. Tostig Raeda's face was
pale underneath his flame-red hair. "What was that?"

"Troll," wheezed Garth as soon as he'd caught his breath.

"Come down from the hills with the thaw. It's laired up under the bridge."

Will looked at the rushing water. *The river's going to be cold,* he thought. *And the current's fast. And that thing in the water has enough strength to pull down a full-grown horse.*

"We can't let it go on living here," he said reluctantly. It was one thing to risk going back onto the bridge in the excitement of the moment, and quite another to plan a deliberate attack, even without Master Finn's words ever-present in the back of his mind: *You can take up the sword and be Sir William Odosson all your life long—but you'll meet death before any other title comes to you.*

"This is the main road north to Strickland from Delminster," he went on. "The next time someone tries to cross the Samsach, they might lose more than just a horse."

He looked down at the sword balanced in his right hand, weighing it. "Anyone here ever fought trolls before?"

The others all shook their heads.

"Right," Will said after a moment. "Let me think, then."

He walked cautiously forward to the bank of the river. No ripple or eddy showed in the swift-flowing water to mark where the horse had gone, or where the troll lurked. The horse was probably down in one of the deep pools, wedged under a rock or a tree root where the troll had hidden it to rot. Trolls preferred their meat soft. And the beasts themselves, so Will had heard, could remain underwater for hours.

Behind him the others were quiet. He wondered briefly if it was his rank as heir to Restonbury that made Garth and the squires defer to him—or was it because he'd been the one who went back onto the bridge after Garth had gone down?

I might have died then . . . but I didn't have time to think that far ahead. So now I have to go on as if I hadn't thought about

*it at all. But drowning in chain mail . . . that's a cold and nasty
way to die.*

Then he shook his head. What he feared didn't matter; he'd
taken the sword from Duke Anlac in the full knowledge of his
own wyrd. He turned and strode back to where the others waited.

"I've got something that may work," he said. "Garth, can you
fight?"

"I'm well enough."

"Fine." Will looked at the two squires. "Seamus, you hold
the horses. If things go badly, ride to the next town and tell the
people what happened. Tostig, you come with us into the water
upstream. We'll form a line and start wading down toward the
bridge. As soon as somebody flushes the troll, we can all jump on
him at once."

"Why not just wait until he gets hungry again and ambush
him on shore?" Seamus asked.

"That could take days," said Will. "And we have to make it to
Strickland before the start of the tourney."

Garth drew his sword. "Then we might as well get on with
it. The water isn't going to get any warmer while we're talking."

Leaving Seamus behind, they walked well upstream from
the bridge and waded out into the Samsach. Will took his place
in midstream, with Garth to his right and Tostig to his left. Icy
water lapped at his thighs, and a strong current pushed against
his legs, trying to force him under.

"Ready," he called. "Here we go."

They started downstream, poking with their swords at the
bottom of the riverbed like blind men feeling their way. The
foam of the river's passage over the rocks made it difficult to
see beneath the surface. Underwater the dim shadows twisted
and joined, and any one of them could be a troll.

The bridge drew closer. Will discovered that he was having a hard time swallowing. His throat was dry and his mouth felt as if it had been stuffed with wool.

"Oh, blast it," Garth said, off to his right. "I've found my horse."

Will looked in Garth's direction. The knight was jabbing at something beneath the river's surface, in a spot where exposed tree roots thrust out from the steep rocky bank.

"Look sharp," Will called. "The troll won't be far away."

As he spoke, something grabbed him hard by the leg and pulled. He fell, barely able to drag in a last gasp of air before the frigid water closed over him. He kicked backward at whatever had grasped him and felt his spur strike something soft.

His sword wouldn't swing underwater, but he could still thrust with it—and thrust he did, sometimes encountering resistance and sometimes not. Through it all he tried not to panic at knowing he was in the grip of something that could tear the leg off a horse. Then the water above him turned dark, and he knew that he was drowning.

Abruptly the grip on his leg broke. Will got his feet back under him and pushed up to the surface. He shook his head to clear the water from his eyes and the hair from his face, and looked around, gasping.

He stood underneath the arch of the bridge; the darkness had been its shadow on the river below. A few feet away his friends had something cornered. Its thrashing movements churned the water into a mass of white foam that Garth and Tostig struck into again and again.

Will turned and began slogging back toward the action. It was twice as hard walking against the current, and he had to lean into the flow. He wished that he had worn his helm; right now Garth and Tostig weren't paying much heed to how they swung their swords behind them. Then he was glad that he hadn't worn it—the extra weight on his head would have drowned him for sure.

He gave a shout to warn the others that he was coming through and brought his own sword down into the foaming water. He felt a shiver of impact as the blade hit something. But the sword rebounded as if it had struck a yielding piece of wood rather than biting into meat.

Over on the shore Seamus hadn't been standing idle. The squire had hitched a couple of the pavilion guy-ropes to the packhorses and fastened a loop to the other ends. Now he tossed the loop into the water, where red bloodstains floated on top of the white foam, and pulled it free. The loop came up empty.

"Try it again!" Will shouted.

Again Seamus tossed his loop. This time the rope went taut and quivering, and water sprayed from it in every direction.

Now Will could make out a shape under the water at the rope's end—a brown, long-limbed creature. "You've got it!" he called out to Seamus. "Now pull!"

Under Seamus's urging, the horses slowly drew the troll forth from its watery home, and all the while Tostig and the knights cut at it with their swords. At last it came up on the shore, still fighting, reaching out fast and hard with its grasping hands, until Tostig pulled a battle-ax from his saddle-bow and struck the creature a two-handed blow. With that it stopped fighting and lay still.

The dead troll was a little smaller than a man, but with arms twice as long as its body and fingers that ended in wicked claws. The head was round, with no ears to speak of, and with small eyes set close together. The lower jaw was massive with muscle, and the mouth gaped open in death to reveal a double row of conical teeth.

So that's what a troll looks like, Will thought. He sat down with his back against a tree, feeling limp and shaky now that the fighting was over.

"Somebody build a fire," he said finally. "I'm cold."

They dried themselves out at the fire, then dragged the troll's body off into the underbrush and left it for the scavenger birds.

"Let vermin eat vermin," said Garth. He looked down at the troll, split nearly in two by the stroke of Tostig's ax. "It's dead and it's going to stay that way."

The rest of the journey to Strickland passed without incident, though Garth had to ride his charger. Late one afternoon, a week after crossing the Giants' Bridge, Will and his friends set up their pavilions beside the tourney field. They were about to turn in for the evening when footsteps approached their campfire.

"Hello there!" called a voice out of the darkness. "Are you the knights from Restonbury?"

"We are," Garth replied. "I'm Garth of Orwick, a Nordanglian knight in service to Baron Odo, and you sound like one of my countrymen. Come forward so we can recognize you."

The stranger approached—a big, black-bearded man who wore a white bear embroidered on his red tunic. "Restonbury's a far ways from the northland," he said.

"That's true," Garth admitted, "but you won't find any lord more chivalrous, north or south."

"Then here's to chivalry," said the newcomer, taking the cup of wine that Tostig held out to him. "Sir Beorn of Stanburh, at your service."

"And I'm at yours," said Garth. "Allow me to make known to you my comrade-in-arms Sir William Odosson of Restonbury. Will's a Southron, knighted just this fortnight past by Duke Anlac himself."

Beorn looked impressed. "That's not something that happens to every sprig of the nobility," he said to Will, "not even in Suthanglia. The duke must hold your father in high regard."

Will felt his face reddening a little. "All I know is that Restonbury has always been loyal to Duke Anlac."

"That's a good enough reason for Anlac to favor you," said Beorn. He drank the last of his wine and handed the empty cup back to Tostig Raeda. "Well, I must be off. I'll see you at the feast tomorrow night, if we don't meet on the field."

After he left, there was silence for a while. Finally Seamus looked up from banking the campfire for the night and asked, "What do you suppose *he* wanted?"

"To find out who's going to be fighting tomorrow," Garth answered. "That's good news for you, Will—everyone will know you're a baron's son, just knighted by a duke, so the ransom they can ask for beating you will be high. You'll be right there in the thick of things, with a better chance to gain glory and win prizes than all the rest of us put together."

Or a better chance to die, Will thought in spite of himself, and he shivered.

            The next morning dawned wet and misty but not quite raining, for which Will felt a certain thankfulness. Nobody liked to fight in mud, but an overcast sky would spare everyone the sweltering burden of full armor on a bright sunny day. On the road he'd worn nothing more than a long coat of chain mail, with a shield for one arm and his sword for the other, but today he armed himself as if for war: a coat of mail; plate-metal vambraces to guard his forearms and solid greaves to protect his legs; his sword and his shield; and a heavy barrel-shaped helm.

By the time Seamus and Tostig Raeda had fastened the last of the straps and buckles on Will's armor, he carried almost seventy pounds of iron weight. Holding the barrel helm in the crook of his arm, he stepped out of the pavilion. Outside, his warhorse was waiting—not Grey Gyfre, but the heavy charger that had been one of his father's gifts to him at his knighting.

Will mounted after checking the girth-strap, bridle, and bits. If he took a fall during the heat of the tourney, he couldn't expect Garth's luck. The great warhorses didn't know the difference between a pitched battle and knightly sport, and were trained to rear and trample the fallen underfoot; in the heat of battle they couldn't tell one knight from another.

Once in the saddle, he put on his helm and rode off with Garth toward the tourney field. A crowd of knights had already gathered, some with crests of red cloth fastened onto their helms and others, like Will and Garth, with blue.

"The first knight I take, I want his palfrey for a ransom," Garth said as they rode. "I'm not rich, and there's no other way I can find a saddle horse as good as the one I lost back at the Giants' Bridge."

Will chuckled. "Well, good luck to you. Just don't forget which side you're on and capture me by mistake."

A horn sounded near the Earl of Strickland's pavilion, and a herald with the earl's device on his tabard stepped out onto the field. The knights all fell silent.

"Hark to the rules of combat!" the herald shouted. "There

shall be two zones of safety on the field of battle—one here at the pavilion of my lord of Strickland and one at Strickland Castle. There shall be no combat within these zones, nor any prisoners taken, nor any parole given. The melee shall last until all the knights of one side are vanquished, or until one side retires from the field, or until the ninth hour, whichever shall occur first. And he who captures the greatest number of knights shall be the honored guest at our feast tonight!"

Another horn sounded, this time far away, from the walls of the castle, and the herald cried out, "Let the tourney begin!"

A great shout rose up. Will and the other knights spurred forward. They thundered across the springy turf, heading for the stand of trees that separated the two ends of the tourney field. Will kept a lookout for knights wearing red crests, but the size and weight of his helm made it impossible for him to glance very far to either side, and its narrow eyeslit restricted his field of vision to a thin strip.

Then, not far away, Will spotted a knight on a great plunging steed. The knight was riding alone, uncompanioned by friends or supporters, and he wore on his helmet the red mark of the opposing side.

"That one's mine!" Will shouted at Garth. To make his meaning clear, he flourished his sword and turned his charger's head toward the strange knight. As he did so, he saw the device painted on the man's shield—a white bear on a red background.

"Beorn of Stanburh!" Will called out, louder this time. He rode straight across the other knight's path, clashing his sword against his own shield by way of salute. "Beorn of Stanburh! You're mine!"

Sound and movement together caught Beorn's attention. He dipped his spear in response to Will's challenge, then couched the weapon again and urged his steed into a charge.

Will brought his horse around to meet the attack, then leaned forward in his saddle, trying to get as much of his body behind his shield as he could. Unlike Beorn, he carried no spear. In this first passage of arms he would have to take Beorn's attack with no way to return the blow.

He gripped his sword in his right hand and rode at the other knight, guiding his steed with his knees. With his left arm he held his shield so that the surface would meet Beorn's spear at an angle, sending the blunted wooden point slanting harmlessly by.

If he'd misjudged, of course, the spear would hit him straight on, with all the weight of Beorn and Beorn's charger behind it. And then, even if his armor held, Will would go out of the saddle for sure, and down beneath the feet of the horses.

No time now to think about that—the gap between him and his opponent was closing too fast. Closer and closer Beorn came, until Will could see the clods of earth flying up from under his charger's iron-shod hooves. The point of Beorn's spear grew larger and larger. Will fought the impulse to change the angle of his shield. Even if he'd judged wrong, his safety now lay in holding firm.

At the last instant Will swung his sword leftward and down into the shaft of Beorn's spear, just before the point slammed against his shield so hard that his teeth rattled. The impact rocked him backward in his saddle with his whole body vibrating like a plucked bowstring. But even through the crash of the collision he heard a splintering noise and a tremendous crack of breaking wood—Beorn's spear had snapped in two where the sword-blade hit it.

Will let out a yell of pure delight. Not even in practice had that trick ever worked so well.

The horses thundered past each other. Will brought his steed back around to face the way he had come, and reined to a halt.

Then he dismounted. If Beorn of Stanburh was an honorable knight, as he seemed to be, he would disdain to take the advantage of fighting from horseback against a man on foot.

Will brought his shield up in front of him. Looking out over its metal rim, he saw Sir Beorn pulling his charger into a turn only a few yards away. For a moment Will feared that he might once again have to face a mounted opponent, but Beorn threw aside his broken spear and swung down from the saddle.

Warily the two knights approached each other. All around them the melee had broken up into a host of single combats like their own. Shouts, hoofbeats, and the metallic clamor of swords and armor filled the air. For Will, however, the uproar soon faded. All his concentration centered on Sir Beorn.

The big knight was good and experienced; his blows came in fast and hard. Will blocked the strokes with his shield as they descended. At the same time he faked a blow to Beorn's head— counting on Beorn to lift up his shield for protection and then drop it again when the expected blow didn't fall.

The first part of the trick worked: Beorn raised his shield. In the brief moment when its rim blocked Beorn's vision, Will struck at his leg.

Beorn must have expected something of the sort. He fell back a pace so that the blow passed harmlessly by, then snapped his sword around before Will could recover his guard. For a while after that Will was too busy defending himself to worry about making any more clever attacks.

The fight settled down into a routine of blow, block, and counterblow that went on for a long time. Some minutes passed, then Beorn stepped back and held up his hand.

Will lowered his sword a little. "Do you yield?" he called out to Beorn.

"No," shouted the other. The thick iron of his closed helm

made his voice sound hollow and blurry. "But I'd like a chance to catch my breath. This is warm work."

Will realized that he, too, was sweating and breathless. "It certainly is," he said. "Let's rest together."

He laid his sword down on the turf and pulled off his helm for a gulp of fresh air. Now that he could see more than a narrow band directly in front of his nose, he realized that the fighting had taken them almost into the woods.

A few feet away, Sir Beorn also put down his sword and took off his helm. Leaning back against a nearby tree, the big knight sank down until he was almost sitting on his heels, then let out a long sigh of relief.

"You fight well," he said. "To be honest, I never expected you would give me such good play. Tell me—how are things in Suthanglia these days?"

"Peaceful enough, as long as the Old King stays alive," Will replied. "My father isn't expecting any trouble this summer. If he were, I wouldn't be here."

"I suppose not," Beorn said. "But Anlac of Delminster has interests up on the border, and you're the duke's liege man just as much as your father is. You can't blame a northerner for being curious."

Will wiped the sweat from his forehead with the back of his hand, and decided that half the truth would serve his purpose. "I have my own reasons for traveling north," he said. "I want to visit Harrowholt and meet my future wife."

"Ah, yes," said Beorn. "Baron Henry's daughter, I suppose. A handsome girl, if you like them dark-haired. Too quiet for my taste. Says odd things sometimes."

Will felt a stirring of curiosity. "You've met Lady Isobel?"

"Now and again," said Beorn, "when I've been a guest at Harrowholt. Baron Henry keeps up friendly relations with his neighbors on the Nordanglian side of the border." The big knight looked thoughtful for a moment. "In fact, I'd heard . . ."

Beorn's voice trailed off, and Will remembered Duke Anlac's words in the dark courtyard—*"Some of my northern vassals, I fear, are perhaps not as loyal as they should be."*

Before Will could ask any questions, however, Beorn pushed himself to his feet, picked up his sword, and put back on his helm. "We can talk about Harrowholt and Duke Anlac tonight at the feast—right now I'm rested enough to fight some more. Are you ready?"

Will replaced his own helm and retrieved his sword. "At your pleasure."

They fell to again. The brief rest had helped Beorn, but it had helped Will even more. He pressed Beorn hard, and the other knight's blows came ever more slowly. Soon Will had Beorn at sword's point, with the tip of his blade leveled at Beorn's eyeslit. A small movement would send it thrusting home.

"Now, sir knight," Will asked formally, "do you yield?"

"That I do," said Sir Beorn, with equal formality. "And it is my joy to have been captured by such a gallant knight. What ransom do I owe you?"

Will thought for a minute. He wished he knew more about the man he had just defeated. Horse and armor—or their price in gold—were a common ransom for a man of Sir Beorn's rank, but some knights could better afford to pay than others. A landless knight might own nothing besides his warhorse and his tourney gear, and Will had no desire to impoverish anyone.

"You know your own worth," he said finally. "Pay me whatever ransom you think is fit. Now go tell the heralds how our contest went. You have your parole."

"I'm on my way," Beorn said. The big knight mounted and rode off through the woods.

Will also remounted, and rode out onto the field. His day had certainly started well: one ransom already and the morning still young.

By the time the horns sounded at the ninth hour to end the tourney, Will had captured four more knights—two of them men he knew well enough to ask for a full ransom without fear of leaving them penniless, and all of them experienced fighters—without once being defeated. Exhausted but in high spirits, he made his way to where the squires were waiting.

"What's the news?" he asked as he dismounted and gave the reins of his charger to Seamus of Ierne.

"People are calling you a new champion," said Tostig Raeda with a grin. He scooped up a dipper of water from the open barrel that stood nearby and held it out to Will. "They say you took four knights."

Will took the dipper gratefully, drinking part of the water and dumping the rest over his head. The sweat of a day's hard fighting had soaked his hair and matted it flat under his helm, and the cool water felt good against his overheated skin.

"Five," he said to Tostig. He filled the dipper again as he spoke, and drained it before continuing. "I counted five."

"I didn't do badly myself," Garth said, coming up behind Will. "I got the horse I was hoping for, anyway. Maybe you counted one of yours twice. I've done that sometimes."

Will passed the dipper to Garth. "You could be right," he said. "But I'll check with the heralds to make sure."

"Good idea," said Garth. "If they're wrong, you've got another ransom coming."

With the aid of Tostig Raeda, Will removed his tourney armor and put on a fresh tunic. Then he went off to the Earl of Strickland's pavilion to consult with the heralds. There he learned that his captured knights had all reported their defeat promptly, except for Sir Beorn. No one had seen him at all since the first part of the morning.

Then the last few heralds returned—the ones who had gone out beating the thickets for those knights who hadn't heard the signal—and one of them had Beorn of Stanburh draped across his saddle.

Will hurried over, fearing that the big knight had been overcome by the heat inside his heavy armor. But as Will drew closer, he saw that such was far from the case. Beorn of Stanburh wasn't heatstruck—he was dead.

chapter
6

"How could something like this happen?" Will asked the herald. "Sir Beorn was alive and in good health when we parted this morning."

"You could say he died from riding through woods in a closed helm," said the herald. "He got knocked out of the saddle by a tree limb he didn't see coming, and his neck broke when he hit the ground." The herald gave Will a speculative look. "Was he a friend of yours? Because somebody has to take him back home to Stanburh for burying."

Will shook his head hastily. "No, no. I never met him before last night. I defeated him in the melee, that's all—he was probably riding back here when he fell."

The herald looked displeased. "Well, if you need the ransom I can't give it to you. You'll have to get it from his friends, if you can find them."

"I don't want the ransom," said Will. He turned away, feeling gloomy and somewhat disillusioned. Maybe the herald had never known the dead man either, but he still shouldn't act as though he blamed Beorn of Stanburh for dying on purpose to ruin the tourney.

Back at camp he found that the bad news had preceded him. "It happens sometimes," Garth was saying to the squires, who were looking a bit quieter and more sober than usual. "Haven't you heard Father Padraic's sermon on the evils of tourney fighting? He preaches one every spring."

"Sermons are for the chapel," Will said as he joined the group. "It wasn't the fighting that killed him. It was a tree limb that any of us could have ridden under, if we'd been the unlucky ones today."

"You think too much," Garth told him. "Trust me—it's a bad habit to get into. We'll drink to Sir Beorn at the feast tonight and say a prayer for his soul in the morning, and that's the end of it."

Will knew that Garth was right. War and fighting were a knight's business. But a small voice in the back of his mind persisted in reminding him that it was easy for Garth to talk. He'd never had Master Finn look into his future and see only death waiting for him.

The image of Sir Beorn's lifeless body draped over the herald's saddle stayed with Will the rest of the day. He and the others cleaned themselves up as best they could in a bucket of cold water and put on their good clothes for the evening feast. Will wore the blue-and-gold velvet from his knighting—the tunic and cloak were a bit crushed and waterstained but fine enough for a knight-errant following the tourneys.

Late in the afternoon they all went up to the castle together. Strickland was a large fortress with square towers and high, thick walls. Restonbury would have looked small beside it, and even Duke Anlac's main stronghold in Delminster, while larger, was scarcely as formidable.

"Are all the castles in the north as tight as this one?" Will asked Garth as they entered the courtyard.

The Nordanglian knight hardly glanced at the structure. "This? Up on the border, they're stronger still."

"We haven't had a war with Nordanglia since my grandfather's time," protested Will. "What are people still building walls like this for?"

Garth shrugged. "Border folk have long memories. Someday the Old King is going to die, and his grandsons and great-grandsons and kinfolk-by-marriage are going to kick the crown of all Anglia from one end of this land to the other. Meanwhile the border lords build strong castles."

In the great hall, the light from the high, narrow windows shone in bands of gold through the woodsmoke. Torches at the lower level illuminated the rush-strewn floor. Shields and banners lined the walls above the trestle tables, interspersed with the age-browned skulls of elk, bears, and unicorns.

The unicorn skulls in particular interested Will. He moved away from the other knights to look more closely at the largest of them. Unicorns were elusive beasts; he'd never seen one, although he'd heard tales of their cunning and their ferocity when cornered. This one's skull was partway between a horse's skull and a deer's in size and shape, with a long spiral horn growing out of the forehead.

"A beauty, isn't it?" said a voice beside Will. "Belonged to the second-largest unicorn I've ever taken."

Will looked around at the speaker. The Earl of Strickland stood there, one hand resting on his belt. Will bowed.

"Good day, my lord."

"And good day to you," said the earl. "You're Odo's boy, aren't you? How are things at Restonbury these days?"

"Well enough, my lord."

The earl laughed. "That's enough 'my lords' for one evening," he said. "The heralds tell me you carried the whole field before you today. Your father was such a fighter in his youth—I remember it well. Will you sit at my side tonight?"

"Of course. I am honored."

When the heralds announced dinner, Will went up to the high table and sat at the earl's right hand in the seat of honor. There he found out what had happened to the largest unicorn the Earl of Strickland had ever taken: The horn had been made into a drinking cup for the earl himself. Will had no trouble guessing the cup's true purpose. Everyone knew that a unicorn's horn would discolor in the presence of deadly poison. As the earl said later in the evening—after he'd drained the horn and refilled it several times—"You're going to be a baron yourself, my boy, so you might as well know the worst of it: You can't trust anyone."

"Yes, my lord." Will looked out over the crowded hall, filled with roistering knights and squires, and wondered what it must be like to look on every man as an enemy. *So many ways to die,* he thought. *Do I have to fear this one, too?*

Midway through the feast there was a fanfare of trumpets, and the double doors of the great hall swung open. A herald entered; he wore the Earl of Strickland's colors and carried a small wooden box on a silver tray. Everybody fell silent, and Will realized with some embarrassment that they were all looking at him.

"The tourney prize," said the Earl of Strickland as the trumpets blew another fanfare.

The herald paced with majestic dignity down the length of the hall to the high table and offered the box to Will. Will took it, made what he hoped was a passable speech of thanks, and then sank back in relief as the herald departed. Conversation started up again all over the hall, and Will finally had a chance to look at the box.

He saw nothing particularly remarkable—only a square box not much bigger than his two fists, made of plain wood without any ornamentation.

"Open it," said the earl. "The prize is inside."

Will opened the box and found an interlaced openwork globe carved out of ivory or old bone. When he picked it up, he saw that it was hollow, with another, smaller globe inside the first, and a third globe, even smaller, inside the second. They all turned freely as he moved the sphere about. Someone had threaded a green ribbon through the carving and tied it off into a loop—for ease in carrying the prize outside its box, Will supposed. He tried unsuccessfully to imagine how many hours of patient work had gone into carving the delicate, useless bauble.

"It's very beautiful," he said.

"Yes," the earl replied. "But that isn't its chief virtue. It comes from the kingdom of Prester John, and the carvings are a spell to bring its bearer good fortune."

"Then I'm doubly honored," said Will. "I'll have to leave it behind when I fight in tournaments, though; I wouldn't want anyone to say I took an unfair advantage."

"If you always fight as well as you did today, you won't need it," said the earl. "Keep it for war, or for hunting . . . we'll be going into Strickland Forest tomorrow, if you want to stay here and try it out. You can count on deer for sure, and maybe something better if the luck is working."

Will shook his head. Sir Beorn's unexpected fate still oppressed him—it could so easily have been his own—and he didn't feel right about hunting for sport in the same woods where the big knight had found his death. At the same time, Will didn't want to offend the earl. He chose his words carefully. "My friends may be staying; I don't know. But I'll be riding northward."

A frown started to form on the earl's features. *Now I have offended him,* Will thought, *and he's a man who fears treachery everywhere—who knows what he might do?*

Hastily Will seized on the first excuse he could think of. The truth alone—Master Finn's prophecy, Will's own fears, and Sir Beorn's death—would probably never be enough to convince the earl. "It's a previous obligation," he said. "I have a bride to meet, up at Harrowholt."

The earl's expression relaxed. "So you do, so you do. Well, I understand that. You'd best be off to see her—ladies don't like to be kept waiting, or at least they didn't when I was your age."

Will left the feast soon afterward, before the earl's temper could change again. The next morning he rose early and began gathering his belongings together. His movements awakened Garth, who yawned and blinked at him.

"Hey!" said the Nordanglian. "Where d'you think you're going? It's barely light."

"I'm riding straight on to Harrowholt," said Will. "I have to see Lady Isobel."

"What's the rush? You've never even met the girl."

"I know," said Will. "But last night I told our host that I was leaving, and I don't want him to think I lied."

He made no mention of his other motive—the fear that his wyrd, like Sir Beorn's, might work itself out in some unexpected moment, and give him no chance to make ready. *I have to meet Isobel before that happens . . . easier not to meet her, maybe, but that wouldn't be honorable. I can't make up my mind what to do about her. Maybe when I talk with her, I'll know.*

The sound of their voices had awakened Seamus, who stuck his head out from beneath his blanket and peered at them blurrily. Sandy brown hair stuck out from his head in all directions like wisps of hay.

"What's going on?" he asked.

"Will's riding off to Harrowholt," Garth said.

Seamus looked at Will. "You're not going alone, are you? That's dangerous—you ought to take a squire."

Will smiled a little. "Meaning you?"

"Who else?" said Seamus. "I want to see this paragon of love and beauty you're in such a hurry to meet. And it doesn't suit your dignity to go traveling without a squire. You've got a position to uphold, remember?"

"It must have slipped my mind somehow," Will said. "Come along, then, if you don't mind missing the next couple of tourneys."

"I've seen a tourney," Seamus told him. "I can live for a while longer without seeing another."

Two weeks later, after an uneventful journey, Will and Seamus rode up to the gate of Harrowholt on Suthanglia's northern coast. The castle stood on a rocky headland at the edge of a bay. Across the water Will saw forested hills, with a tower rising up in the distance. That would be Nordanglian territory on the farther shore, he thought, and the tower would mark the castle of Baron Henry's closest neighbor.

Will knocked with his fist on the wooden door beside the castle gate. The small window set into the door at eye level swung open at once, as if the gatekeeper had been waiting for the signal. He probably had; Will suspected that he and Seamus had been spotted from the castle a long time earlier.

"Who comes here?" the gatekeeper demanded.

"Sir William Odosson of Restonbury," Will said. "I'm here at Baron Henry's invitation to meet my betrothed, Lady Isobel."

The gate swung open. Servants came running up to take the two palfreys and Will's charger, and more servants came to unload the packhorses. Will let Seamus oversee the arrangements for their animals and baggage. He himself was too preoccupied in scanning the courtyard for Baron Henry's face.

He didn't see the baron anywhere, or anyone else that he knew. But on the steps leading up from the courtyard to the castle hall, he saw a young woman standing—a girl, really, his own age or perhaps a little younger. She had on a plain gown such as his mother and sister wore when they were working on household tasks, and her dark brown hair was braided into thick plaits that hung almost to her waist.

What struck Will the most keenly, however, was her expression: a mixture of surprise, curiosity, and something else that he couldn't put a name to. He barely had time to say to himself, *That must be Isobel*, before she stepped back into the shadows of the doorway and disappeared.

He didn't see the girl again until that evening, at the feast the castle cook had hastily thrown together in his honor. This time she was dressed in what had to be her best gown, made of dark blue velvet embroidered in gold. Her long hair was loose and wavy under a floating veil of thin white silk.

Baron Henry of Harrowholt beamed with pride as he led his daughter up to the high table and seated her next to Will.

"It's time you two youngsters became acquainted," he said. "Will, this is my girl Isobel. Isobel, this is Sir William Odosson of Restonbury—Baron Odo's heir and as promising a fighter as I've ever seen. He vanquished two outlaws single-handed while he was still only a squire."

Will rose to his feet and bowed; Isobel curtsied; and Baron Henry, with heavyfooted subtlety, went off to confer with the head cook about the roast pork, leaving the two young people alone and tongue-tied at the high table.

They sat down, and Will tried to think of something to say—no easy task when he could feel everybody in the great hall watching him, from Baron Henry down to the minstrels and the kitchen boys. He wasn't sure what he and Isobel were supposed to be talking about. Except for his sister, who didn't count, life at Restonbury hadn't given him much chance to meet women of his own age and rank.

Isobel was the first one to speak. "Was Father right?"

Will blinked, startled. "About what?"

"About the outlaws. Did you kill them—is that what he meant by 'vanquished'?"

This was not, Will reflected, the conversation he'd thought to have when he left Strickland. "It wasn't a tourney," he said. "They would have killed me."

She looked at him from under level dark brows with an expression he couldn't interpret. "Why did you fight them?"

"There was an old woman," he said. "They were trying to steal her pig. I told them to stop, and they wouldn't, so we fought."

"And you won."

Will was silent for a moment, remembering the blade of the outlaw's sword flashing down through the sunlight, and the moment when he was sure that he, and not his enemy, would be the one to die. "Yes," he said finally.

"Father was going to take me to Saint Edwiga's," she said, "to watch you fight in the tourney. He said I would enjoy it."

The change of subject startled him, but tourneys at least were something he could talk about. "I don't know," he said. "When I was a squire, all I could see from the sidelines was a big cloud of dust with swords waving around in it."

Isobel laughed—a warm, pleasant sound, in contrast to the grave expression she'd worn since he first saw her. "What's it like on the inside of the cloud?"

"Exciting," he said after a little thought. "Dangerous, but exciting, like a game. The real thing is different."

Isobel hesitated for a moment. "I suppose it must be," she said at last. "Did you miss very many tourneys, coming to Harrowholt early like this?"

Will nodded. "The one at Barren Hill, for certain, and maybe Wendyke. But I ought to be back with the Restonbury knights by Midsummer at Saint Edwiga's."

"Where you were supposed to be meeting my father and

coming here," Isobel said. The laughter had gone out of her voice. "But you came early. Why?"

Will looked away. "I don't know . . . it's hard to explain." He forced himself to look squarely back at her. "We have to talk," he said. "Without all these people watching us. Is there anywhere—"

Before he could finish his question, a horn blew. A whole roast pig emerged from the castle kitchens, its platter borne on the shoulders of a pair of sturdy manservants.

Tomorrow, thought Will, as a roast swan reclothed in its natural plumage followed the roast pig, and a baked carp followed the swan. *I can tell her about Master Finn's prophecy tomorrow. She looks like a sensible girl . . . if she says it doesn't matter, then maybe I won't have to worry about breaking the betrothal contract after all.*

chapter
7

The feast ended with the presentation of a castle made out of spun sugar and gilded gingerbread. Baron Henry, Will decided, must be either greatly loved or greatly feared by the cooks of Harrowholt, to have them provide such a feast at short notice. Will hadn't eaten so much at one meal since Restonbury, and was glad to retire early to one of Harrowholt's tower chambers, where he slept deeply and without dreams.

He woke the next morning to the sounds of a disturbance in the castle—footsteps rushing back and forth outside the chamber door, hoofbeats down below in the courtyard, and a deep voice that sounded like Baron Henry's shouting orders that Will couldn't quite make out.

He flung aside the covers and rolled out of bed. His good tunic was hanging from a wrought-iron peg set into the wall. More important, if trouble had come to Harrowholt during the night, his sheathed sword was hanging close beside it. He pulled the blue-and-gold velvet over his head without bothering with belt and hose, and took down the sword.

Already he heard footsteps coming up the spiral stairway to his room—a heavy, urgent tread. Carrying the sword sheathed in his left hand, he padded barefoot over to the chamber door and flung it open. The noise that had sounded like half a score of attackers turned out to be Baron Henry and a middle-aged woman in servant's garb. The woman was sobbing; Baron Henry was red-faced and breathing hard.

"What's wrong?" asked Will. "Has something happened?"

"It's Isobel," said Baron Henry. "We've searched the castle without finding her—if she isn't in here with you, she's gone."

Will fastened his swordbelt around his waist in a series of quick, automatic motions. The familiar weight at his side reassured and steadied him, letting him speak to Baron Henry in a voice that sounded calmer than he felt.

"I've been alone all night," he said. "Are you sure she's gone? This is a big castle—there must be lots of corners where a girl could lose herself if she wanted to be alone for a few hours."

The baron glanced at the servant, who Will suspected was Isobel's old nurse. "Oh no, sir," the woman said to Will. "She had places, but none so hidden I couldn't find her if I tried. I looked in them all before I wakened my lord baron."

Will frowned. "Could she have slipped out early in the morning to—to gather herbs or some such thing?"

"She'd never have gone alone," the woman said. "There's too many outlaws and ruffians about. No, sir, she's vanished, and I say it smells of magic."

"Gytha's right," said Baron Henry. "My Isobel's been magicked out of Harrowholt somehow. All the gates are still barred, and no one saw her go past."

"What about your enemies?" Will asked the baron. "Could one of them have done it?"

"Nobody on this side of the border hates me that much," Baron Henry said. He thought a minute and added, "Nobody on the other side, either, as far as I can tell. They're sworn to King Morcar in Orwick, and I'm sworn through Duke Anlac to the Old King in Tamsbrycce, but we're all friendly in spite of that."

"Maybe not as friendly as you thought," said Will. He shivered.

A coldness against the soles of his feet and a draft blowing against his shins reminded him that he was standing barefoot and barelegged in an open doorway. "Let me get the rest of my clothes on, and I'll join the search."

He closed the door and went over to the chest where Seamus had stored his clothing yesterday evening. The blue-and-gold tunic he'd snatched off the peg wasn't meant for riding out in all weathers. Since he had to get hosed and shod anyway, he might as well put on something more suited for the task at hand.

He unbuckled his swordbelt, then took off the velvet and folded it away. After a moment's consideration he pulled out a plain linen tunic and a pair of woolen hose. Something fell out of the folds of cloth as he lifted them. It was the wooden box that held the prize from the Strickland tourney.

On an impulse Will opened the box and took out the ivory globe. He considered the bauble thoughtfully.

"The carvings are a spell to bring its bearer good fortune," the earl had said.

Will wasn't sure if he believed that or not. Saying an object was enchanted was a good deal easier than making it so, even for earls and wizards. But if he was going to go out hunting for a lost girl, he could use all the luck he could get.

He slipped his white leather belt through the loop of ribbon so that the bauble hung next to his dagger. Then he strapped his sword back on, thrust his feet into stout rawhide boots, and went downstairs in search of Seamus and a horse.

His path to the stables took him through the great hall, now dim and cheerless. The benches and trestle tables had been taken apart and shoved against the walls so that servants could clear away the scraps and litter from last night's feast. Baron Henry stood in the middle of the hall, arguing with a shorter man who wore the dark, hooded robe of a wizard.

"I have finished my conjurations, my lord," the wizard was

saying, "and it's just as I suspected. I detect no trace of magic strong enough to kidnap Lady Isobel."

"But you're not denying there's magic about!"

The wizard heaved a patient sigh. "My lord, there is *always* magic about. If it isn't some kitchen-maid using one of her grandmother's cantrips to make the butter churn faster, it's a stableboy reciting charms to calm down the horses. Wasted effort, most of it—a spell without power behind it is just empty words—but in a place this size you're bound to find one or two people with a touch of the wizard's gift."

Will cleared his throat, and the two men broke off their conversation. The wizard bowed curtly, first to the baron and next to Will, and then strode off, his black robe flapping around his ankles. The baron shook his head.

"I don't know why I fool myself that he knows anything," Baron Henry muttered.

Will couldn't think of an answer to that, so he said only, "With your permission, my lord, I'll ride out now and join the search. Which direction should I take?"

"The main parties rode west and south," Baron Henry said. "You'll have to hurry if you want to catch up."

"Yes, my lord," said Will. He bowed and hastened on down to the stable. Seamus was already there, with Grey Gyfre saddled and bridled.

"I heard the news," said the squire, "and I thought you might want Gyfre. He's the better horse if what you're thinking of is a long day in rough country, with a good brisk chase at the end of it." Seamus paused and looked at Will hopefully. "Do you need me to come with you?"

"Why not?" Will started to say. But the encounter with Harrowholt's wizard had called up memories of Master Finn and his prophecies. "No," he said finally. "You can't tell what might happen. If I don't come back in a sennight, take the warhorse and my tourney armor and go meet Garth and Tostig at Saint Edwiga's."

Seamus looked troubled by Will's request. "What's all this about 'if I don't come back'? You haven't—"

"Foreseen my own death?" Will shook his head. "No." *Not in the way you're thinking of, at least,* he added to himself, and went on aloud, "A wise man prepares for everything, just in case."

"If you say so," Seamus said. "But God willing, you'll find the damsel safe in a meadow somewhere, stringing the morning flowers to make you a love garland."

"Maybe," said Will. But he didn't think it likely. Even in the brief period he'd known her, Isobel hadn't seemed like the garland-stringing sort.

He put on his armor—not the full tourney gear, but the coat of mail that he'd worn on the road, with his shield and an open helmet. Then he mounted Gyfre and rode out.

The day was clear and bright, with a brisk wind blowing. Will scanned the horizon in all directions for any sign of the men from Harrowholt. West and south, Baron Henry had said the main search parties were riding. Will paused, looking out to see if any of the searchers were in view.

As he hesitated, considering, a flicker of motion to the north caught his eye. Something white, it had been, too far away for him to make out clearly, moving across the dark background of the trees. A young girl in a white shift, perhaps, or a rider's white horse . . . or a white deer, like the one that had led him astray in the woods near Restonbury.

As omens and portents go, he thought, *I've heard of clearer ones. But it will do.*

He turned Gyfre's head to the north. When he reached the spot where he'd glimpsed the white deer—or whatever it had really been—he found a narrow road leading away through the trees. He looked at the road, trying to see it as kidnappers might, or even a young girl traveling it for reasons of her own.

No dead trees blocking the way, and no grass springing up in the wagon ruts, he thought. *This isn't just a forest trail—it's the high road to Orwick. Why isn't anybody searching along it? Is Baron Henry that sure of his northern border? Or is there something up there he fears to disturb?*

In either case, Will reflected, it seemed odd. Maybe Baron Henry was right, and there wasn't any need to search in the direction of Nordanglia. But somebody ought to be looking up that way, just the same, in case the baron was wrong.

Nobody else is searching in this direction. If Isobel is somewhere in the north country, I may be the only one who can find her.

The day grew warmer as Will rode on beneath the rustling trees. Even this far north, the bright green leaves of spring had begun to fill out into the darker foliage of early summer. The arching boughs cast dappled shadows on the road, making dark and light patterns that shifted with the changeable breeze.

In late afternoon, he came to a river with a wooden bridge over it—no giants' stonework here, just thick timbers cut square and pegged together. A shield bearing the arms of the king of Nordanglia hung from a pole a spear's cast beyond the bridge. Shortly after the river crossing, the trees began to thin out into open ground. Will heard a sharp whistle off to his right. When he looked, he saw a sheepfold tucked into the edge of the woods. A shepherd was directing his sheep into their cote with the help of a large black dog.

"Ho—shepherd!" Will called out. "Whose land is this?"

The shepherd gazed at Will for a long while before answering. Finally he said, "Grimmersfell's."

"Lord Grimmersfell's?" Will asked.

The shepherd spat into the dust of the sheepfold. "Aye. Baron Edric of Grimmersfell."

"Have you seen a young girl pass by here? Or men on horseback carrying a young girl among them?"

"Might've been something making my sheep nervous this morning before light," said the shepherd. "Or might not. I couldn't say."

Will thanked the shepherd. The man's vague air of hostility puzzled him, though it hadn't seemed directed toward Will himself. The shepherd probably had some kind of minor grievance against the baron, Will decided, riding on.

Soon a stone tower loomed up over the plowed strips of the village fields. After a moment's thought Will realized that he was looking at the same castle whose tower he'd seen from Harrowholt the day before, the stronghold of Baron Henry's closest neighbor to the north.

Good, he thought with relief. *Baron Henry said they were friendly. I can tell them about Isobel and ask for help.*

As he drew closer, he saw that Grimmersfell was a small castle, of rough appearance but stoutly built. In one section of the curtain wall, the stonework had been replaced by a heavy wooden palisade—not as pretty a repair as a stonemason could do, but faster and less costly.

A man-at-arms holding a pike guarded the gate. At Will's approach, he lowered his pike to block the way and called out, "Who comes?"

"Sir William Odosson of Restonbury," Will replied. "Have I come to Grimmersfell?"

"That you have, sir knight," said the man-at-arms. His voice was thick with the accent of Nordanglia. "Wait here."

Before long the guard returned. "Come in, sir knight," he said. "And be welcome."

Will dismounted and led Gyfre through the gate. Inside, the courtyard was small but clean, with hard-packed earth underfoot. Except for the curtain wall itself and the stone tower in the center of the courtyard, Grimmersfell was built of wood: the wellhouse on one side of the yard, the stables and outbuildings, and the long, high-gabled hall.

Will frowned. The villagers at Restonbury built in wood, and some of the more prosperous ones, like Thurstan the Shire-reeve and his family, lived in cottages almost as large as this castle's hall. But wood burned, or decayed, and had to be rebuilt; Will could recognize new work when he saw it. All the wooden structures in Grimmersfell's courtyard had been put up at the same time, and now that Will knew what to look for, he could make out the dark smudges of soot stains blackening the outside of the tower.

A fire, he thought. *And not so long ago. Less than a year. The price of building in wood, I suppose . . . but a fire that took the buildings and left the tower standing shouldn't have taken down the stonework of the outer wall.*

He puzzled over this while a second man-at-arms took his horse and a third escorted him to meet the baron. In the hall, servants were setting up tables for the evening meal. A knight not much older than Will himself sat in the High Seat—a stocky, dark man with a thick black mustache. He was drinking wine out of a plain metal cup.

"Welcome to Grimmersfell, sir knight," he said as Will approached. "I am Edric Ingeldson, Baron of Grimmersfell."

Will remembered his manners and bowed. "I am Sir William Odosson of Restonbury, my lord."

The man's dark eyes lit up with interest. "Restonbury? Then you're Suthanglian—one of the Old King's men."

"I'm sworn to Anlac of Delminster," Will said. "But it comes to the same thing."

"While the Old King's alive, at least," said Baron Edric. "Stay with us tonight, Will Odosson; it's been a long time since we've heard news from as far off as Restonbury."

Will saw his opportunity and took it. "There's news from just across your border in Harrowholt," he said. "The baron's daughter has been stolen away by mischief or by magic, and it's my search for her that brings me north."

Edric looked shaken at the news; he drained his cup of wine and set the empty goblet down hard on the tabletop. "Lady Isobel is gone?"

"Yes," said Will. The baron's reaction surprised him a little, until he recalled that Edric was not a stranger to his closest neighbor, even with a border in between them. "Taken, or wandered astray . . . no one is sure. I'm searching along the northward track."

"The woods around here can be dangerous," said Edric. "They're no place for a man to travel alone. Stay here with us tonight, and my men and I will ride out and join the search at first light tomorrow."

One of the servants escorted Will from the great hall to a small chamber in the castle's central tower. Grimmersfell's hospitality was somewhat rougher than Harrowholt's; the room held only a narrow bed and a low, three-legged stool. The servant went away and came back a few minutes later with a jug of water and a basin. He set the basin on the stool, put the jug on the floor beside it, and left.

Will poured some water into the basin to wash his face and hands. While he was scrubbing away at the sweat and road dust, a church bell started ringing somewhere nearby. The insistent summons reminded Will that he had not been to Mass since he left Restonbury—not good, in a world where death and misadventure waited for everyone.

He followed the voice of the bell and found himself in the Grimmersfell chapel, a narrow stone room built onto the side of the tower. An elderly priest was lighting the candles on the altar as Will entered. A moment later, the rest of the castle's knights and Baron Edric entered in a group.

A young page rang a small silver bell, and the Mass began. Will followed along, responding as Father Padraic had taught him, until the time came for the sermon. The priest crossed over to the pulpit, genuflecting before the altar as he went, and looked out over the little congregation.

"Dearly beloved," he began, his voice holding a strong accent of Ierne, "today I will speak of Saint Dismas."

Baron Edric scowled. Behind him, his household knights stirred restlessly, as if they wanted to move but dared not. Will had always liked the story of Dismas, the repentant thief who made a good death and found a welcome in paradise, but the lord of Grimmersfell chewed on the ends of his mustache and glared at the priest until the sermon ended.

I wonder why he dislikes the story so? Will wondered. *Does he think a foreigner might believe that Grimmersfell's priest is calling its baron a thief?*

After the sermon the priest turned back to the altar to continue the rite. Will knelt. The silver bell rang again. Then, as the priest partook of the bread and wine, the Baron of Grimmersfell stood, and all his knights with him, and stalked out of the chapel.

Will remained alone, kneeling, until the end of the Mass—no more than a few minutes. Afterward, as he walked across the courtyard to the great hall, he pondered over what had happened.

Baron Edric and the chaplain of Grimmersfell didn't seem on the best of terms at the moment. From the way the baron and his knights had behaved during Mass, that sermon about Saint Dismas had been a deliberate message, with a meaning both Edric and the chaplain understood. Possibly, Will speculated, Edric thought the priest was asking him to give the church too much, for charity's sake, while the priest thought that Edric was giving too little. A good lord and a good priest could have such a disagreement, and it wasn't a guest's place to interfere.

Will shrugged and went on into the hall to join the rest at dinner—a hearty meal, though simply cooked. Afterward he made his way to the chamber that had been given him, and slept. But something about Grimmersfell made him uneasy: He slept in his mail coat, and kept his sword by his side.

chapter
8

Will awoke early the next morning. The east wind blew in over the windowsill, bringing with it a smell of fish and salt water from the nearby ocean, and the mail coat he'd slept in weighted him down. He rolled over and pushed himself up to sit on the edge of the low bed. He pulled on his boots, then picked up his sword from the floor where the weapon had lain—sheathed but easy to hand—all during the night.

Rising, he fastened the swordbelt around his waist and put on his cloak, then looked out the window. Below him in the courtyard a party of mounted men was already gathering. Baron Edric had not forgotten his promise to search for the vanished Isobel. Will retrieved his helmet and shield from the corner and went down to join the hunt. Grey Gyfre waited for him in the courtyard, already saddled. He mounted and rode out with the men of Grimmersfell into the early morning.

Rain had fallen during the night, and a light fog curled up in tendrils from the pools of standing water. The overcast sky grew lighter as the group of riders broke up into twos and threes and headed for the forest to the south. Will found himself riding in the company of a burly, red-faced knight whose name, he learned during their first few minutes of idle conversation, was Ohtere.

"What makes your lord think we'll find Lady Isobel on this side of the border?" he asked the Nordanglian knight after they had separated from the main hunt. "Grimmersfell is a long way from Harrowholt for a girl on foot."

"But not for a man on horseback," said Ohtere. "And the forest is full of outlaws and masterless men. If she strayed too far away from home, they'll have got her for sure."

Will thought about Isobel in the hands of men like Osbert of Orkney and Hywel de Galis, and his mouth tightened. "In Suthanglia, the shire-reeves hang up outlaws by the roadside as a warning against things like that."

"If my lord knew for certain where these outlaws laired," Ohtere said, "we'd have burned them out a long time ago. But the peasants around here know more than they're telling." The knight gave a harsh laugh. "We'll have it out of them now, though. When they shelter kidnappers, they've gone too far."

Will frowned. He disliked Ohtere's talk of forcing answers out of the common folk of Grimmersfell. *Maybe it's necessary. He knows how matters stand here, and I don't. But something's wrong in a barony when the people favor thieves and murderers over their own lord.*

Aloud, he said only, "We still don't know for sure that Lady Isobel's been kidnapped."

"My lord is sure," said Ohtere, and then fell silent, as if Baron Edric's certainty answered all questions.

After that Will and Ohtere rode for some time without speaking, following a trail that ran along the forest's edge. They came at last to a sort of crossroads marked by a stone pillar. A small path, too narrow for more than one rider at a time, led away from the main track into the deep woods.

At the foot of the pillar, a spring bubbled up into a stone-rimmed pool. Ohtere nodded toward the spring. "Saint Cuthberd's Fountain," he said, his tone halfway between reverence and local pride.

Will crossed himself. He'd heard the tale of Saint Cuthberd from both Master Finn and Father Padraic, although Master Finn claimed that the martyred hermit had been a solitary wizard and not a priest—"For how else," Finn said, "can we explain the fate of those who killed him?"

Meanwhile Father Padraic insisted, with equal vehemence, that no magic was needed when the prayers of the righteous were answered. But Cuthberd's last words had certainly held power of one kind or another: The pillar marked where sea-raiders had nailed the murdered hermit's head to a wooden stake, just before wind and lightning came down from a clear sky to smite the reavers dead and smash their boats to kindling.

Ohtere pointed at the trail that ran into the deep woods. "We'll hunt that way," he said. "Keep alert—some of the outlaws use bows. If you don't look sharp, the first sign you have that they're near is when you get an arrow in your eye."

Will glanced around nervously and wished that he hadn't left his closed helm behind at Harrowholt with the rest of his tourney gear. As time passed and no arrows came winging out of the undergrowth, he grew less uneasy, though no less watchful. He had just begun to suspect that the forest was completely deserted when he spotted a peasant woman gathering firewood a little way off the path.

Will lifted a hand to point her out—but before he could speak, the baron's man drew his sword with a whoop. "There's someone who can tell us what we want to know!" Ohtere exclaimed, and spurred his horse forward. "Come on!"

The woman dropped her bundle of sticks and ran.

Ohtere rode after her, sword in hand. The mounted knight quickly overtook the fleeing woman—a girl, really, not much older than Isobel, in ragged garments of drab homespun wool—then wheeled his horse around and backed his quarry against the trunk of a tree. He swung down from the saddle and advanced on the woman, with his sword pointing at her throat.

"She's hiding something," he said over his shoulder to Will. "They always are. We'll find out what she knows fast enough, once we start tickling her."

Ohtere placed the point of his sword at the hollow of the woman's neck, with just enough pressure behind the blade to dimple the skin. She made a frightened noise deep in her throat. Will's stomach churned.

"Stop that," he said. His hand was on the hilt of his sword, and he drew it as he spoke. "Ask her questions if you have to, but don't torment her."

"What's it to you?" said Ohtere. "In these lands, she's mine to do with as I want."

He drew back his arm to strike at the woman. Will, still mounted, pressed Gyfre forward and brought his sword down into the path of Ohtere's blow. The two blades clashed and held.

"I told you," said Will, over the locked swords. "Leave her be."

Ohtere snarled. "Are you preaching at me, boy? I'll give you a sermon you won't forget in a hurry!" He pulled away and swung at Will's leg—a nasty blow, meant to hamstring and cripple. Will caught the blow on his sword as Gyfre spun in place, then brought his blade back up and down again toward Ohtere's shoulder. Ohtere blocked, but not fast enough, and Will felt his sword edge biting through the linked mail into the flesh beneath.

Ohtere dropped his sword and fell to his knees. Bright red blood welled up from the gash in his shoulder. He clasped his left hand to the wound, with his now useless right arm hanging limp. More blood ran down between his fingers and dripped onto the turf. The peasant woman stared at him for a second, wide-eyed, then took to her heels and ran.

Will slid down from the saddle. He let go his sword and caught Ohtere just as the kneeling man collapsed.

"I'm sorry," Will stammered. "I—"

"You've nearly killed me," Ohtere said. The high color had gone from his face, leaving the skin greyish white. "Why did you have to do that?"

Will shook his head. "I didn't mean—I was afraid you were going to hurt the girl. She'd done you no harm."

"Only wanted to put a scare into her," Ohtere muttered. With a sudden effort, the knight wrenched himself around and fixed his gaze on Will. "She's one of the outlaws, or else she knows where they are. We'll never find Harrowholt's girl now—she's lost for good."

"I'm sorry," Will said. "I thought . . . I don't know what I thought. But you shouldn't have used a helpless woman so."

Then he shook his head. Fine words wouldn't hide the fact that he'd wounded one of his host's own men—maybe killed him, if Ohtere didn't get back to Grimmersfell in time. And waiting wasn't going to make things any better. He lifted Ohtere to his feet and put his shoulder under the man's un-injured arm.

"Here, up on your horse. We have to get you home."

He was helping the wounded knight back into the saddle when the high, clear note of a horn sounded in the woods off to the east. A moment later the breeze shifted, and he heard shouts and the ringing of metal. The horn sounded again.

Pale as he was, Ohtere straightened in his saddle. "That's fight-ing," he said. "Somewhere close by. Baron Edric is in danger, and I have to help him."

"You need to help yourself first," Will said. "You're wounded, and you're still bleeding."

Ohtere pulled away and gathered up his reins in his left hand. "We both know how that happened," he said. "What'll you do if I don't go back to the castle—kill me?"

He rode off in the direction of the fighting. Will stood for a moment, biting his lip. Then he picked up his sword, remounted the patient Gyfre, and followed after.

He didn't have far to go. Just over the next rise, two groups of men on horseback fought each other with grim seriousness, nothing like the games of the tourney. Ahead of him, Ohtere was already riding into the press. Will marked where Ohtere had gone, and plunged after him into a tumult of noise and furious motion.

For a few seconds nobody in the melee noticed Will's passage. Then a man aimed a blow at his head, and Will blocked it with his shield before Gyfre carried him past.

Still following Ohtere, he rode on into the mass of armored men, blocking and defending himself against attacks from all directions. He struck no blows of his own, since he didn't know Baron Edric's people well enough to tell friend from foe with any certainty. He'd already half killed one man from Grimmersfell today, and that was enough.

A knight on a black horse rode toward Will, sword upraised to strike. A closed helm concealed the rider's face, but the device on his shield—a leaping stag in silver against a green background—was nothing Will had seen before. Nevertheless, Will countered first one attack from the stranger, and then a second, before risking a stroke of his own.

The rider on the black horse threw off Will's blow with his shield and struck again. The stranger was fast; Will found himself hard put to block in time and wasn't surprised when his next two attacks were met as easily as his first.

In spite of the deadly earnest of the combat, Will began to feel a kind of sharp, fierce pleasure in the exercise. Not even in the melee at Strickland had he found himself matched against such an adversary, a splendid fighter who could stretch his own abilities to the utmost. It was almost a pity, a detached part of Will's mind observed, that one of them was going to die before the contest was over—probably him, and then the wyrd Master Finn had seen for him would have come to pass.

His duel with the strange knight continued unchecked. None of the other knights in the clearing intervened. Instead they drew away from the single combat, giving Will and his opponent more room. Will pushed forward, moving in closer despite the fact that the black charger was bigger and stronger than Grey Gyfre—but Gyfre was steady and unflinching, thanks again to Restonbury's master of horse, and Will's blows were at last starting to drive the other knight back.

Without warning the stranger pulled away. For a moment he did nothing, only regarded Will from within the concealing mask of his helm. Then he turned and spurred off into the forest.

Will started to follow, then thought better of the impulse. Chasing alone after a fleeing enemy was a good way to get yourself killed. He reined Gyfre to a halt and looked to see if any Grimmersfell knights were close enough to join the hunt.

And saw no one. The woods were empty, and he was alone under the shadowy trees. The melee had passed beyond him, or else he had ridden clear through it in the course of his combat with the strange knight and now had no idea where he was.

Turning Gyfre, he followed the horse's trail of hoofprints and broken underbrush back to where the fighting had taken place. The clearing was silent: no horn calls or clashing of arms, nothing but the wind in the trees. He found trampled grass and patches of ground cut up and stirred into mud, but no living sign of what had just happened.

After some thought, Will decided to ride south. Such a course would bring him to the river that marked the boundary between Harrowholt and Grimmersfell. From there he could find the road back to one barony or the other—although after what he'd done to Ohtere, his welcome at Grimmersfell might not be of the warmest.

He soon realized that his earlier searching, coupled with his pursuit of the strange knight, had taken him further afield than he'd suspected. For several hours he rode, guided by the sun, without coming out of the trees, until he realized at last that he wouldn't reach Grimmersfell or any other lodging before the daylight ended.

Will sighed. It was going to be a long night—no fire, in case the flame should betray him to the outlaws, and no food, since he had expected to be dining again with Baron Edric in Grimmersfell's hall. And cold, but as long as no storm winds blew in from the sea to the east, cold he could endure.

Will hobbled Gyfre and set the horse to foraging nearby. Then he wrapped himself in his cloak, put his back against a tree, and sat half-dozing as the shadows lengthened.

He must have slept, because when he woke up—with a start that knocked his head against the tree trunk behind him—the forest was dark, an unrelieved blackness broken only by scraps of starlight visible through the branches overhead. He looked around, trying to spot whatever had wakened him.

Nothing, at first. And then, just at the edge of his vision, he spotted a bluish light bobbing and weaving among the trees. He tried to look at the flame directly, but whenever he gazed at the light straight on it flickered and vanished.

Faery-lanterns, Will thought, crossing himself. No matter how strong the urge to see where such lanterns might lead, no good ever came to anyone who followed those pale, wavering flames.

He closed his eyes against the flickering light. Being fated to die, he reflected, didn't mean he was eager for it. He would not be led so easily to his doom.

For a long time he held his eyes shut. When he opened them again, however, the light was not gone. It was nearer now and coming closer, moving from side to side like a lantern swinging in a man's hand. But the color of the light was all wrong for a lantern. No candle made on earth had ever burned with such an unstable, blue-white flame.

Will drew his sword as quietly as he could and held it up so that the quillons and the grip made a cross before him.

The light became easier to see as it drew nearer. No longer a flicker glimpsed out of the corner of his eye, it was in the open now—sometimes obscured by the trees as it passed among them, but always there. Always there, and coming straight toward him.

Still holding up the sword in front of him, he eased himself to his feet and made his way quietly to Gyfre's side. He silenced the horse with his hand and undid the hobble.

He didn't dare mount, knowing what tree limbs in the dark could do to an unwary man who rode in the woods. Instead he stood motionless, with Gyfre's reins clutched in one hand and his sword held up before him in the other.

The faery-lantern drew closer, weaving in and out among the tree trunks. Its blue gleam reflected against the polished metal of Will's upraised blade. Then the light emerged from the trees, close enough now that Will could almost touch it.

He would have gasped, but the breath caught in his throat. The faery-lantern was a lantern in fact, and Beorn of Stanburh was carrying it.

chapter 9

Will stood his ground even though his whole body shook. Not since Master Finn had come to him in the chapel at Restonbury and told him he was doomed had he experienced anything like this: the cold, crawling, marrow-of-the-bone fear of something that neither skill nor strength could turn aside.

The dead man came closer. An arm's length away he stopped and lifted up his ghostly lantern so that its pale blue light shone onto Will's face.

Will bit his lips to keep from crying out. If Beorn touched him, he thought, he would have to break and run, or else go mad.

But the ghost only looked at him by the light of the upraised lantern and did nothing. Finally Will forced himself to speak.

"What do you want from me? I never harmed you, Beorn of Stanburh—we fought a fair battle at Strickland, and you yielded to me of your own will."

The ghost did not answer.

"What do you want?" Will demanded again. "You were never my enemy. You spoke to me kindly during the tourney, and we would have talked more afterward, if you hadn't—"

He broke off. The dead man was beckoning to him. The ghost made the gesture a second time and then vanished. A moment later, the flickering light of the faery-lantern appeared again among the trees some distance off.

This time Will followed it. *Sir Beorn meant well toward me while he lived*, the young knight told himself. *And he died owing me a ransom. If it's the weight of his obligation that disturbs his rest, I owe him the chance to pay the debt.*

Still leading Gyfre by the bridle, Will went where the lantern guided him. It was dark under the trees; twigs caught in his cloak and in his horse's gear, and the brush rustled and cracked beneath his feet. When the blue flame of the ghost-light disappeared, he thought for a moment that he had followed it for nothing after all.

Then Will saw a red glow between the trees up ahead. He moved closer and saw a fire burning in the midst of a circle of huts and lean-to shelters. He paused. If this was the sort of place he suspected, his presence might not be welcome. But Beorn's lantern had guided him here; if he'd trusted it so far, he supposed he should trust it a little further.

He sheathed his sword and stepped out from the trees into the edge of the firelight. "Peace be to all here," he said. "I'm a stranger in your forest and I've lost my way. In charity's name, I ask for shelter until morning."

No voice answered him, and no one came out to meet him. But when he drew nearer, he saw a woman sitting on a log facing the fire, so that he could see no more of her than the long hair falling down her back. He thought at first that he'd found the peasant girl over whom he and Ohtere had come to blows. Then she rose and turned to face him—not the girl from the forest, after all, but Isobel of Harrowholt in a plain homespun gown.

"Hello, Will," she said. "You shouldn't have come looking for me."

He shook his head. "I had to—your father sent out riders everywhere, and I couldn't stay behind."

"I understand," she said. "But it doesn't make any difference. I'm safe here and I'm not going back."

Will looked around the clearing. All the huts and shelters appeared empty and deserted. "Who are your friends—and where have they gone?"

"People of the woods," she said. "They have other places. A guest of Baron Edric's isn't going to see them."

"Are they the ones who took you from Harrowholt?"

"No—I took myself." She returned to her place by the fire and gestured at Will to take a seat beside her. "You can't stand there all night," she said. "Come sit down and get warm."

Will turned Gyfre loose to nibble at the grass around the edges of the clearing and seated himself on the log. He clasped his hands together and looked down at his knuckles. "You should go home," he said.

"I can't."

He glanced up at her. "You said you were among friends. Who's forcing you to stay?"

Her eyes were dark and steady, framed by the wavy curtain of her long brown hair. "If I go back to Harrowholt, they'll make me marry you."

"Oh," he said, stung, and looked away. "Is the thought of marrying me really that bad?"

"No. But I don't *want* to marry anybody at all."

"You're the heir to a barony," he pointed out. "You have to marry someone. Even if your father agreed to let you stay unwed, Duke Anlac would never allow it."

"I know," she said. "When you came to Harrowholt, I thought you brought the duke's command for our wedding."

Will laughed without much humor. "Just the opposite," he said. "I came to tell you that you shouldn't marry me."

She was frowning now, a thin line between her eyebrows. "And how is your 'shouldn't' different from my 'won't' in the eyes of our lord the duke?"

"I haven't spoken of this to Duke Anlac," said Will. "Or to anyone else until now. But the day before I was knighted, my father's wizard favored me with a prophecy: I'll never live to be the Baron of Restonbury."

Isobel didn't say anything, but he heard her breathing catch a little. Her expression hadn't changed. He twisted his linked fingers together and stared down at them again.

"I wanted to talk to you," he said, "because I didn't think it was fair—that you should have to marry me, and come to Restonbury, and get nothing out of it besides widowhood." He paused. "Would that be so bad, though? Duke Anlac would have trouble forcing you to marry a second time, if you told Father Padraic and Master Finn that you'd sworn an oath not to. A widow can do that, it's her right—and then you could go on as you pleased."

"You do have a kind heart," she said. "But I've chosen my own way. You'll have to go back to Harrowholt alone."

"I can't lie about finding you," he said. "And your father is certain to ask. Are you sure you won't come with me?"

"Yes," Isobel said.

Will gazed into the fire. If Isobel were truly determined not to go back, he couldn't think of any way to bring her with him to Harrowholt except by force—and even if he'd been willing to try something like that, there was no guarantee that her mysterious friends were as far off as she claimed. On the other hand, he felt reluctant to leave her without any protection except those same unseen allies.

Then he remembered the Earl of Strickland's ivory bauble. It had brought him good fortune of a sort: He'd found Isobel, and he'd come unhurt out of both the fight with Ohtere and the melee in the woods. Even Beorn's ghost had not harmed him, but had aided him to what he was seeking. He untied the loop of green ribbon from his belt and held out the carved ivory globe.

"Here," he said. "This is for you. It brings luck."

She shook her head. "I won't take your luck away."

"I haven't had it long enough to start depending on it," he said. "It was the prize at Strickland. Take it—you need the good fortune as much as I do, and it's too pretty a thing to be worn with a coat of mail."

Isobel took the bauble, though she still seemed more unwilling to hurt him by refusing than eager to accept. She held it for a moment between her hands, turning it about and following how the nested spheres moved inside each other. Will thought he saw her expression change. But she said nothing, except to thank him and tie the loop of green ribbon to her own belt.

Then she stood. "Rest by the fire, Will—you've ridden a long way, and the night is cold. Tomorrow morning is early enough for you to decide what you will do."

She moved away into the shadows. Will sat by himself with his cloak pulled around his shoulders, watching the red lights shifting and running like salamanders in the burning logs. After a while he heard a woman's voice singing somewhere in one of the shelters.

> *"My mother got it in a book,*
> *The first night I was born,*
> *I would be wedded to a knight*
> *And him slain on the morn."*

Will thought sleepily that he should have found the words disturbing. But the warmth of the fire spread over him, and the flames hissed and crackled underneath the sound of the woman's singing, and try as he might he couldn't keep his eyes open.

"The King he has a daughter fair
And young and shrewd is she,
Knows all that in the world is wrought,
And all that e'er shall be."

Will felt his eyelids growing heavier as he listened to the song, and presently he slept.

He woke to sunlight dappling his face through the canopy of green leaves. Gyfre stood over him where he lay wrapped in his cloak on the ground. Rising and stretching muscles cramped from sleeping on the cold earth, he looked about the clearing. He was alone, and more than alone—the huts and shelters he had seen last night were gone. He saw no sign of a camp and no footprints other than his own.

A chill ran down his spine. *Was last night all a dream, then—Beorn and Isobel both?*

He shook his head, dazed. That *couldn't* be what had happened. He had watched the fire for a long time, while somebody sang. The firepit, at least, was still here.

He went down on one knee beside the ring of blackened stones and felt for any trace of remaining heat. Nothing—the stones were cold, and the logs had burned down to ashes.

A day, maybe two, since this burned, he thought. His hand shook a little as he brushed the fine grit off his fingertips. *Have I been bewitched and lying here for two days?*

It seemed impossible—he was hungry, but nowhere near as hungry as a three-day fast would have left him. Nevertheless, the ashes in the firepit would not lie. He got back up to his feet and let his hand fall to the pommel of his sword. His fingers touched nothing but empty air. The heavy wooden scabbard wrapped with leather was empty, and the blade was nowhere in sight.

"Saint Cuthberd protect me," he muttered, crossing himself. "This is powerful magic."

He raised his voice. "Isobel!"

Nobody answered. If an outlaw camp had ever been hidden in the woods around this clearing, it was gone now.

Will called out, "Isobel!" again, and then gave up. He might be weaponless, and Isobel might be long away in the company of her elusive friends, but he still had a duty to return to Harrowholt and report what he had seen.

He mounted Gyfre and rode eastward, finding his direction from the shadows the sun cast on the ground below the trees. He hoped that he wouldn't meet anyone else along the way—either living or dead—so long as he didn't have his sword. The blade might be, as Master Finn had foretold, his key to an early death, but without it he felt bare and helpless.

He rode for some time unmolested as the morning wore on. When he emerged from the woods, however, he saw that he was not south of the boundary between Nordanglia and Suthanglia, as he had thought, but north of it. The castle walls he saw in the distance were those of Grimmersfell.

Will shook his head. *I'm better off leaving that place behind me,* he thought. *Not everything there is as it should be, and Ohtere isn't likely to have given the baron a good report of me, either.*

But almost as soon as he'd left the forest a horn sounded from within the castle, its pale call torn by the wind and trailing away on a high note. Soon after, the gate opened and a group of armored knights rode out. Will reached for his sword, remembering too late that the scabbard was empty.

He sat taller in his saddle as the mounted band covered the half mile or so from the castle gates, and prepared himself to be seized and taken prisoner. To his surprise, however, the knights did not attack. Instead the leader of the group, a knight Will didn't recognize, rode up beside him.

"We thought you were dead, along with Ohtere," the knight said. "Come back to Grimmersfell with us, and we can take care of your wounds."

Will blinked. "Wounds?"

"There's blood all over your surcoat," said the knight.

Ohtere's blood, thought Will, but now didn't seem like the time to say so. He blinked again and said vaguely, "There was some fighting—I've lost my sword."

The knight drew his own blade and held it out to Will pommel first. "It's not good to ride about unarmed these days," he said. "Here, take mine."

Will's fingers closed around the grip of the sword. The feel of it in his hand reassured him, even though it was only a common blade and not a finely crafted weapon like the one Duke Anlac had given him.

"What about you?" he asked the knight.

"Don't worry," said the knight. "I won't be helpless." He pulled a mace from his belt. "This is more than enough to keep off the local vermin."

They went back to the castle at a slower pace. Will kept silent during the ride. This was not a good time to betray his confusion by asking the wrong questions. Soon the half-ruined and hastily repaired walls of Grimmersfell drew near. The troop rode under the portcullis and into the courtyard, and Will tried not to flinch as the heavy wooden gate slammed shut.

One of the castle grooms came up to take Gyfre away. Will felt a strong reluctance to hand over the reins to a stranger, even though everybody in Grimmersfell had so far treated him as a friend. He swallowed his unease and went with the other knights into the timber-built great hall. The narrow, high-gabled building was dark inside. No fire burned in the long central hearth. The only light came from two branches of thick white candles on either side of a rough trestle table at the far end of the hall.

Sir Ohtere lay on the splintery planks between the candles, his body wrapped in a sheet of bleached linen, his face set in the pallid waxiness of death. Baron Edric and the Iernish priest stood at either end of the table, facing each other down its length with Ohtere's body laid out between them. From the anger on Baron Edric's face and the narrow, obstinate line of the old priest's mouth, the two men had not been interrupted in the midst of prayers.

Will shook his head. The quarrel between Baron Edric and the chaplain of Grimmersfell was none of his concern. Sir Ohtere, however, was. The body of the dead knight drew his eyes no matter how he tried to look away, and he half expected the shrouded form to sit up and accuse him where he stood.

And rightly so, the voice in the back of his mind pointed out. *He's dead, and it was my arm that struck him down.*

Will swallowed hard—recognizing the truth was not the same as liking it. Quickly, before his resolve could fade, he strode down the length of the hall to where the baron stood.

"My lord baron, there is something I must tell you," he said. "This is all my fault."

The baron cut him off with an abrupt gesture of one hand. "This isn't the time to quibble over shares of the blame," he said. "You and Ohtere both did your best. He's dead, and we mourn for him; you're alive, and we can rejoice over that."

Will opened his mouth and shut it again.

Ohtere never told him about our fight in the clearing, he thought in amazement and relief. He looked at the table again and swallowed. There was only one thing left to do.

Will turned to the Iernish priest. "Father," he said, "I'm a wandering knight, a rider from tourney to tourney, and it's been a long time since I confessed my sins properly. Will you hear them?"

The priest nodded—but the glance he threw at Baron Edric looked oddly triumphant.

"I will hear them," the old man said, turning again to Will. "In fact, I have been waiting to do so. Come with me to the chapel, sir knight, and we will do what needs to be done."

chapter
10

Will followed the priest out of the great hall into the courtyard. The bright glare of midday had softened into the golden light of afternoon, and their shadows stretched out long on the packed earth. Once they were beyond earshot of the hall, the priest slowed his pace and looked over at Will.

"Shall we go into the chapel?" he asked. "Or is that a little too close to heaven for what you have to say?"

Will frowned. The question made him uneasy. Baron Edric's chaplain was talking in riddles that would do a wizard proud— just one more thing wrong in a barony where nobody, highborn or low, was behaving as he should.

"Let's go to the chapel, Father," he said. "I want to confess my sins to God, not to you."

"Very proper," said the priest. "You're a credit to your teachers, whoever they were. But the chapel is for matters of the next world. It's the work of this world you need advice on, young man, and quickly, too."

Will halted. "I said I would make my confession in the chapel. The open yard isn't a proper place."

"Don't be so stiff-necked, boy," said the priest. "You can't afford it. You killed Sir Ohtere, didn't you?"

Will said nothing, but something in his eyes must have given him away. The priest's expression softened.

"Oh, don't worry," the old man said, his tone more kindly. "I'm not a prophet, or a wizard either. I see what passes before my eyes, nothing more. A man rides out of Grimmersfell whom I know to be cruel and violent beyond even his fellows, and that man dies of a sword stroke. Three days later his companion returns, spattered with blood that's not his own. And that same proud pious young knight, who had every chance to be shriven when he first came to this castle—that same knight wastes not a breath before asking the way to God's forgiveness."

"You're—"

The priest held up his hand. "Be careful. What I hear outside the confessional I must in law tell the baron."

"I'm not up to playing at riddles, Father," Will said after a long pause. "That's a game for wizards and not for men like you and me. If there's something that I need to know, then for the love of God tell it to me now."

"Listen, then," said the priest. "Baron Edric wasn't born to the lordship of Grimmersfell. A year ago, at midsummer, he took the castle by force. And by treachery—the fire of the castle's burning must have been seen in Harrowholt, and I know a messenger was sent, but no help came."

"How do you know all this?"

"I saw the old Baron of Grimmersfell send out the messenger myself," said the priest. "And I was here when Edric's men threw down the curtain wall and broke into the tower. I stayed alive only because no one among them dared to kill a priest in front of his own altar. Not in this district. Saint Cuthberd's memory stays too green for that."

Will nodded slowly. The priest's story accounted for a number of strange things about Grimmersfell, from the fresh timberwork to the unspoken quarrel between the baron and his chaplain. But—"I've never heard anyone say that Henry of Harrowholt was a false friend."

"You have now," said the priest, his eyes hard and bright with remembered anger. "Listen again. That missing daughter of his was betrothed to you. Her father also promised her to Grimmersfell, while she was just an infant—and now Baron Edric is claiming that the lady should belong to him, along with the castle and the title, by right of conquest. And Baron Henry has never said him nay."

Will didn't know what to think. He wanted to disbelieve the old priest's story—Baron Henry had treated him with courtesy during his brief stay at Harrowholt—but he feared that it was true. And Isobel, who didn't want to marry anyone at all, was promised not twice but three times over.

"No wonder she ran away," he said, half to himself. "But who could she find to take her part? Where could she go?"

"North," said the old priest at once.

"Why north? Why not south, to her own overlord and the king in Tamsbrycce, and ask for justice there?"

"Because she's not stupid, boy," said the priest. "Duke Anlac's behind most of what goes on in this part of the world. Her father is the duke's man, and so are you—and so is Edric of Grimmersfell, in spite of the border. If the girl went south with her tale, the duke would have her father's head for promising her without permission to a Nordanglian lord. And then Anlac would marry her off anyway."

"To me?" Will asked. "I'm the duke's man in everything that's honorable—but I don't want a bride who's unwilling."

The priest's mouth gave a craggy twitch that Will supposed might be a smile. "Your duke might not share those scruples," he said. "And Harrowholt's daughter would never have trusted him, not when she has uncles and cousins in the north—her dead mother's kinfolk—and friends as well. Look to the king at Orwick; she'll be heading there.

"And now, good sir, come to the chapel and I'll hear your confession. We've been away long enough—Baron Edric will think there's a conspiracy brewing if you don't reappear soon."

Dinner that evening at Grimmersfell was bleak and dreary. Will and Baron Edric sat at the high table, while the rest of the knights and the men-at-arms sat at trestle tables in the lower hall. The servants had carried Ohtere's bier to the chapel for the funeral and burial after sunset, and they had kindled a new fire on the central hearth, but the changes had not lifted the gloom from the atmosphere.

Will ate little and spoke less. He kept turning over in his mind the idea that Baron Edric, a Nordanglian who had taken another Nordanglian's land by force, was also the sworn man of a Suthanglian duke.

If the baron was Duke Anlac's man, then he probably assumed that the duke had sent Will to Grimmersfell—which the duke had in fact done, though not for the reasons Edric probably thought. Or maybe the baron did suspect the truth. How else would a clever man deal with a guest who might be a spy, except give him a warm welcome and whatever help he asked for and tell him nothing?

Will glanced over at his table companion. Baron Edric didn't seem to have any more appetite than Will did; he had left untouched the slices of roast pork on the trencher before him and sat moodily turning his wine cup around in his hands.

Is he Duke Anlac's traitor? Will wondered. *He's already betrayed the king in Orwick by swearing fealty in secret to a Suthanglian duke. Is he ready to turn his coat back again? And for what?*

Or should the duke look for his traitor in Harrowholt instead?

Will didn't like the way his thoughts were tending. He shook his head to clear the gloom away and turned to Baron Edric. "Those men who attacked your party in the woods," he asked, "who were they? Not common outlaws, if they fought in armor from horseback."

Edric looked glum. "No. But not anybody I recognized, either. And I don't know where they came from."

Will paused. "There's another thing. In Suthanglia, everyone says that magic is stronger and more common here in the north. Is that true?"

The baron shrugged. "There's always magic," he said. "Whether it's stronger in Orwick than in Tamsbrycce, who knows? But if you're saying those knights we fought were just some kind of wizardly phantoms—one of them had a sword that was real enough for Ohtere."

Will looked down at the table. "Yes. But I was thinking of something else. When I was lost in the woods, after darkness had overtaken me, I saw a ghost."

"A ghost."

"A knight called Beorn of Stanburh—did you know him?"

Edric breathed out heavily through his mustache. "He's a good man. I hadn't heard that he was dead, though."

"He died by chance at a tourney in Strickland, about a month ago. We fought fairly and parted friends—I don't know why he should have come back. But I followed him, when I was lost in the woods, and he led me to a forest camp where I found Isobel of Harrowholt."

"You found her and you didn't bring her back?" Baron Edric sounded incredulous.

"I told you, there was magic at work. We talked by the fire and I fell asleep waiting for morning. When I woke up, the fire had been dead for three days or more, and I was alone, with my sword taken from me."

"Isobel was gone?"

"Like everything else from the night before," said Will, "except the ashes of the fire."

Edric looked at Will for a long time, as if trying to search out the truth of his story. "A strange tale," the baron commented finally, "but I won't say it's impossible. We have our wizards and suchlike here in the north, and if one of them is mixed up in all this . . ." He let the sentence trail off into a shrug, and then asked, "Will you be going back to Harrowholt?"

Will shook his head. "I don't know. I think I should follow Isobel, wherever she's gone now, but I'm not sure if I ought to go any farther alone."

"Stay with us tonight then," said Baron Edric, "and see Ohtere buried. You can make up your mind tomorrow which direction you should go."

Staying at Grimmersfell to attend Sir Ohtere's funeral wasn't a prospect Will found particularly attractive, but he couldn't think of any way to escape the unpleasant duty. After the meal ended, he climbed the stairs to the top of the stone tower and looked southward toward Harrowholt, where the towers of Baron Henry's castle shone in the last of the sunlight.

Will stood for some time alone in thought, while the dark clouds blew across the setting sun and a low mist came in from the sea to cover Harrowholt. Something was wrong, not just at Grimmersfell as he had suspected, but in the whole border country. If Isobel had seen it as well—*and she would have,* he told himself; *she's lived here all her life, and being a girl doesn't mean she's stupid*—then she might have run away from Harrowholt not just because of him, but to escape whatever it was that she saw coming.

I wish she'd told me what she was afraid of, he thought. *Maybe I could have helped.* He shook his head. *Now I'm the one being stupid. Whatever she's afraid of, she thinks I'm a part of it.*

Am I?

The thought chilled him. Duke Anlac had sent him north to look for treachery, and if the chaplain of Grimmersfell was telling the truth, treachery he had found.

But Baron Henry had invited Will to Harrowholt even before the duke had laid his commands on him. Maybe the baron's hospitality was only a chance for two young people to meet each other before the wedding ceremony linked them forever. But how could that be, when Baron Henry had already promised his daughter twice over to other bridegrooms?

Maybe Baron Edric had been pressing his claim harder of late. And with the old lord of Grimmersfell dead, Baron Henry might have lost his taste for a Nordanglian son-in-law—especially one who was secretly sworn to Henry's own overlord. Isobel's father would have had good reason, then, to hurry along the original match with the heir of Restonbury. Isobel herself had been afraid that Will's arrival meant an unexpected rush into marriage.

I don't blame her for running, Will decided. *Something very bad is going on up here, and Baron Henry is in the middle of it.*

By the time the sun had dipped below the trees to the west, Will had resolved not to return to Harrowholt at all but to ride directly for St. Edwiga's. Seamus would find him there when he came looking for Garth and Tostig.

Will could find a scribe in St. Edwiga's to write a message for Duke Anlac setting forth what he had learned. With Isobel safe out of the way—wherever she had gone—the duke could make what use of the news he wanted. Will could finish out the tourney season and, if he was still alive at summer's end, go home to Restonbury for the winter.

Feeling satisfied with his decision, Will left the tower and went down the spiral staircase to the chapel. Ohtere's funeral Mass was just beginning. Will entered the dim, candlelit chamber and knelt among the other knights.

"Hello, Will Odosson," whispered the man kneeling to Will's left. "I'm happy to see you here with us."

Will kept his head bowed, but looked sidelong at the speaker and saw only a dark form muffled in a hooded cloak. Then the speaker's head turned, and Will saw inside the deep hood the face of Sir Beorn of Stanburh.

Before Will could speak, another whisper came, this time from Will's right. "Hello, Will Odosson. I also am happy to see you here."

Will turned his head. Another muffled figure knelt beside him at his right hand. This one, too, he recognized: Sir Ohtere, whose corpse lay waxy-pale before the altar where the old priest chanted the funeral prayers.

Will crossed himself and stared down at the pavement, unable to look any longer at the two dead men who knelt flanking him on either side.

The voice of Beorn of Stanburh whispered again on his left. "We fought fairly; I bear you no ill will. Leave this place tonight and ride to Harrowholt."

"We rode out together, and you struck me down." Ohtere's whisper was like a rattle of dry leaves on Will's right. "Leave this place tonight and ride to Harrowholt."

"Why should I—"

Will cut his own low-voiced reply off short when he looked up and saw that he spoke to nothing but empty air. Both Beorn and Ohtere had vanished.

At the altar, the old priest had finished the prayers for the dead. Now the sanctus bell rang, a clear silver note. Everyone else's attention was on the uplifted chalice, lustrous in the glow of the altar candles, and on the pure, repeated note of the bell. The priest lowered the cup and drank.

I can't stay here any longer, Will thought. _Not when the spirits of dead men surround me, all speaking with one voice and telling me to go._

Standing, he pulled his cloak around him and slipped away unnoticed through the chapel door. He went down the stairway and out into the courtyard.

The sunset had faded, but the deep purple twilight of summer let him find the stable and saddle Grey Gyfre without disturbing any of the castle grooms. He put on his armor and made his way to the gate. The main gate of Grimmersfell was shut and barred against the night, but the man-at-arms by the small gate let him through.

"You take care, sir knight," said the guard. "The woods here are strange and unchancy once all the light is gone."

"So I've seen," Will said. "But I'll be well away on the high road before then."

He mounted Gyfre and headed south. By the time the last light of the gloaming had faded, he'd crossed the river at the wooden bridge and was riding deeper into Suthanglia under the milky glow of a sky full of stars.

chapter

11

All night he rode, holding Gyfre to a steady pace. The moon rose and set, and the stars faded again. Just before first light the towers and walls of Harrowholt rose up ahead of him.

The castle gate was shut when Will rode up to it.

"Who goes there?" a guard's voice called from the wall above. "Name yourself!"

"Sir William Odosson of Restonbury!" Will shouted upward into the dark. "Let me in, would you? I've been riding all night. I'm dead tired, and so's my horse."

The gate swung open with a groaning of wood and metal. Will blinked against the sudden brightness of a bonfire that burned in the center of the courtyard. Dark figures moved back and forth against the orange firelight. As Will dismounted and walked Gyfre through the gate, he saw that the shadowy figures were knights and foot soldiers wearing the livery of Duke Anlac.

Will squeezed his eyelids together and shook his head in a vain attempt to clear away the fog of exhaustion. *Duke Anlac . . . here? If there was trouble that bad on the Suthanglian side of the border, there'd have been talk of it up in Grimmersfell.*

One of the knights left the fire and came up to Will. "You there," he said. "Come along. The duke is waiting for you."

That doesn't make sense, Will thought blurrily. *I didn't even know I was coming here myself until after sunset.*

Unless one of the duke's wizards had been searching for him—but that didn't make sense either. He wasn't such an important vassal of Duke Anlac's that his lord needed to waste a wizard's time following all his comings and goings.

Still caught up in the puzzle, Will let one of the castle servants lead Gyfre away. Then he followed the duke's knight up the steps into the great hall. In spite of the hour, the hall was packed with men—armed knights, most of them, with faces among the crowd that Will had not seen since his knighting at Restonbury. A fire blazed in the central hearth, and torches burned in brackets along the stone walls.

A pair of tall, man-high candlesticks stood at the far end of the hall. Their branches of thick beeswax candles made a puddle of clear yellow light in the space between them, where Duke Anlac sat in a heavy, high-backed chair. Will's confusion deepened as he realized that, aside from the duke, he didn't know any of the men in the hall by name.

Where's Baron Henry? he wondered. *This is his hall, not Duke Anlac's . . . and Seamus isn't here either.*

"Take off your sword, Sir William," said the knight who had brought Will in from the courtyard, "and approach the duke."

Will stopped moving. "His Grace gave me my sword with his own hands when I was knighted. Whose command is it that I disarm myself now—yours or his?"

"By the duke's command, Sir William," said the knight. "Take off your sword."

"I am the duke's man," Will said slowly, "sworn to him in all honorable things." He drew his sword—glad now that it was a stranger's inferior blade and not the fine weapon he had received from the duke—and handed it over to the man beside him. "Keep this for me until His Grace tells you to give it to me again."

Then he turned his back on the knight and walked up the length of the hall to where the duke sat waiting. He heard the other man's footsteps following behind him all the way.

"Stop," said the knight suddenly, when Will was still five yards or more from the duke's chair. "Kneel before His Grace."

Will knelt. For a moment past and present seemed to fold together, and he was back in the great hall of Restonbury, waiting to receive the sword stroke that made him a knight.

Then Anlac spoke. The duke's voice rasped harshly, and even by the flickering, unsteady light of the candles Will could tell that he had not slept in a long while.

"Is this the traitor?" the duke asked.

A man stepped forward out of the shadows behind Anlac's chair. "It is," said Baron Henry of Harrowholt.

"My lord, he lies!" Will leapt to his feet, but strong hands clamped onto his shoulders and thrust him down again onto the rush-strewn floor.

Baron Henry kept on talking as if Will had not spoken. "He has been in congress with the Baron of Grimmersfell these four days and more—stealing my girl away from her home and handing her over to those northerners."

"My lord, don't believe him!" Will cried out. "He's—"

A heavy fist struck him on the side of the face. "Silence, you, while His Grace pronounces judgment."

Will's mouth tasted of blood where the blow had driven the inside of his cheek against his teeth, and his ears rang. Before he could draw breath to protest again, Duke Anlac spoke.

"Bind him, take him away, and at sunrise hang him. Treason shall not live in my lands."

The duke stood up and strode out of the hall without looking back. A moment later Baron Henry followed him. Only when the two men had left the hall did the duke's knight drag Will back up onto his feet. Will stood—dazed equally by Baron Henry's accusations and by the duke's belief—while a pair of men-at-arms cinched his hands behind his back, drawing them far up between his shoulder blades with his own white belt.

Then they took him to a small room off the main hall, down a short passage, a room without window or chimney, and threw him into it. The door slammed shut, and he lay sprawled on the floor where his captors had thrown him. Already his arms were growing numb, his shoulders ached, and his eyes stung with tears of shame and anger.

The Earl of Strickland was right, after all, he thought as the first wave of despair washed over him like a flood. *You can't trust anyone. I gave Henry of Harrowholt all the help I could, and he pays me back like this—handing me over to the duke's hangman and shaming me before all Anglia.*

Will choked back a sound that was somewhere between a laugh and a sob. Henry had probably sent word of the "treason" to Duke Anlac himself, or had his wizard do it, the moment Will first arrived at Harrowholt. Anlac couldn't have gotten here so fast otherwise. Which meant that Isobel's father had planned all this as long ago as Will's knighting, and had invited him northward for no other purpose.

If Isobel hadn't run away, Will realized, her father would just have invented some other crime for him to commit. What mattered was that the duke had been looking for a traitor all spring, and Baron Henry had given him one. But that Anlac should believe the baron—and worse, that Anlac should accept the baron's word without letting Will speak in his own defense—for Will, that was a betrayal worse than anything Henry of Harrowholt might have done.

The duke doesn't care whether Baron Henry is telling the truth or not, Will thought. *I've just come from Grimmersfell, and that makes me unsafe. I know that Baron Edric is the duke's man in secret, and I know that the duke has been meddling where he shouldn't have. So my own lord is going to let me die in disgrace, just to keep me from telling anyone else.*

Will groaned. This was a wyrd more bitter than even Master Finn had foreseen—not only death waiting for him, but disgrace as well. Ohtere's ghost would be pleased to see him meet such an end. *And what of Sir Beorn?* he wondered. *Did he speak the truth when he said he bore me no ill will? Or was Beorn lying, too?*

He gave thanks that he had confessed his sins to the priest at Grimmersfell and so would die recently shriven. If his silence was the goal, it seemed unlikely that Baron Henry and the duke would allow him to speak to anyone, even the castle's chaplain, between now and sunrise.

Awkwardly, using only his legs and upper body, Will levered himself into a sitting position and propped himself against the wall. His skull ached, and he could feel his jaw swelling where the duke's knight had struck him, but his arms and hands had long since gone completely numb. He leaned his head against the coolness of the stone and prepared to wait out what little time was left for him.

He was still sitting there when the door to the little cell creaked open. A head appeared, silhouetted against the reflected firelight outside.

"Will, are you in there?"

"Seamus!" Will exclaimed in a hoarse whisper. "What are you doing? Get back to Restonbury before they catch you talking to me and hang you, too. Tell my father it was lies, all of it, that I never—"

"I'm not going anywhere," Seamus cut in. "Not without taking you with me. Come on."

"I ought to make you leave me here," Will said, "but I'm not so eager to die that I'm going to argue about it."

He struggled to his feet and lurched forward. Without the use of his arms for balance, even simple actions like walking became difficult.

Seamus reached out and steadied him. "Here, let me get you out of that."

The squire untied the belt that bound Will's hands and helped him out into the passageway. A man-at-arms lay stretched out across the stone floor. A dark pool of blood spread from beneath his body.

Will halted. "What did you do to him, Seamus?"

"He wasn't going to let me in to talk to you." Even in the scant light that filtered into the narrow passage from the hall beyond, the squire's face was pale enough to make every freckle stand out in high relief. "I thought once I was inside, the two of us could overpower him somehow, but . . ."

"You've killed one of the duke's own men," Will said. "He'll never forgive you for it."

"The duke was about to hang you and ruin your good name," Seamus said. His voice was steadier now. "And *I've* never sworn any oaths to Anlac of Delminster."

The squire pulled a roll of cloth out from under his arm and unfolded it. It was a surcoat marked with the device of Duke Anlac. "But you did—so you can wear his colors a little while longer."

Will let Seamus help him get the surcoat over his head. He still couldn't feel his hands, or even raise them much above his waist, because of the numbness and the cramping.

"That surcoat's not going to help much with the duke's men," he said as Seamus belted the garment around him. "They'll know I'm not with them."

"They're not the ones I'm worried about," Seamus said. "It's

the guard at the gate who mustn't know you, and he's one of
Baron Henry's people."

The squire finished working with the belt buckle and stepped
back. "There. Let's get our horses and be gone."

The great hall was almost deserted
now, and darker than it had been before. The fire in the central
hearth had burned low, and many of the torches had gone out.
Of the great company that had waited there, only a couple of
sleepy men-at-arms remained on guard. Will tensed at the sight
of them, but nothing happened—the combination of a white
belt and Duke Anlac's colors appeared good enough to lull their
suspicions.

"Where are we going once we get the horses?" Will muttered
to Seamus as they left the hall.

"You're the knight, not me," Seamus said. "Once we're outside the walls, I'll follow wherever you lead."

Outside, the bonfire still burned in the courtyard. By its light,
workmen labored at making something out of beams of wood.
Most of the structure lay stretched out on the ground, but Will
could see that it would be quite high when they finished—high
enough to hang a man.

He turned his face away.

The noise of hammering continued as he and Seamus walked
around the shadowed side of the yard toward the stables. Once
there, two more familiar figures came forward out of the dark:
Garth and Tostig, both of them armed and armored.

For a moment Will could say nothing. He was too full of
amazement and gratitude to speak. Finally he found his voice.
"What are you two doing here?"

"Waiting for you," said Tostig. "We were at the Wendyke
tourney when His Grace came through on his way northward,

breathing fire and talking of treason. Since Sir Garth is sworn
to the duke through your father, the two of us didn't have much
choice but to come along." The squire laughed. "When we got
here and heard what Baron Henry was claiming you'd done, we
knew it was nonsense, of course—you're not the conspiring sort."

Garth nodded agreement. "So we're with you, wherever
you're going. Just remember we're all of us the duke's men, except for Seamus; if we hurt Anlac or any of his people, our hon-
or's forfeit."

"You're splitting hairs for my sake already," said Will. "I'll
try to keep you clear of anything worse." He thought for a moment. "We'll head north. Garth has family there, and nobody
can blame him for wanting to go home once in a while."

"It's been a long time since I saw my grandmother in Orwick," agreed Garth. "Let's saddle up and get out of here."

A few minutes later the little group
emerged from the stable, all walking their horses. The sky was
greying overhead, with a rosy tinge over the sea to the east, and
the noise of hammering echoed busily off the walls of the courtyard. In the little while that Seamus and Will had been inside
the stable, the carpenters had raised up part of the scaffolding.
A hooded man in Duke Anlac's livery stood watching them, a
coil of rope slung over his shoulder.

"If the duke wants them finished by sunup, they're going to
have to hurry," Seamus commented.

"They can take their time," Will said. He caught his breath
on the last word, biting his lip against the pain of life coming
back into his cramped hands. After a moment he went on, "I'm
in no hurry to try out their workmanship, you understand."

But the brief hesitation hadn't gone unnoticed. Garth looked
over at him and frowned. "Will you be able to ride?"

"If I can get in the saddle, I can ride," said Will. "But I don't know how long Gyfre can run. He was on the road from Grimmersfell all night."

They drew near the small gate of Harrowholt Castle—the low, narrow entrance beside the great wooden double-doored portal. The guard spotted them and called out, "Who comes?"

"Garth—you answer him," Will whispered. "He knows my voice by now."

"I said, who comes?" the guard said again, more sharply.

"Knights in Duke Anlac's service," Garth called back. "We have urgent business outside the walls."

"Nobody comes or goes, by order of the baron."

"As you wish," Garth said. He drew a little closer. "Then we'll just wait here awhile."

"You can do your waiting over by the fire. Honest business won't go sour before sunrise."

"Here, now—you don't have to talk like that." Garth took another step forward and shrugged his shield onto his arm.

The guard drew his sword. "Trouble at the gate!"

Garth didn't wait for any more. He lifted his shield and punched out with its iron-bound rim, catching the guard in the throat. The man fell.

Tostig ran past the fallen guard and twisted the bar of the small gate from its iron brackets. He heaved at the gate, swinging it open, and the group from Restonbury hurried through—Will first, then Seamus with the horses, and last of all Garth, sheathing his blade.

"So much for trying to slip away unnoticed," Will said. "We're heading north."

chapter 12

They mounted their horses and rode. Will's arms and hands ached fiercely with the pain of life returning to cramped muscles. But the sky was light in the east, and before long the rim of the sun would show above the horizon. He knew that if he'd still been in the cell at Harrowholt, the duke's men would have come for him by now.

They might still get you, he reminded himself. *And if they do, you'll be lucky if they only hang you. One of Anlac's men is dead, and one of Baron Henry's is lying injured at the gate—they've probably both been found by now.*

He looked back over his shoulder at Harrowholt Castle. A low mist hovered above the fields, and the castle walls rose out of the drifting vapor like mountains above the clouds. Dark figures on horseback emerged from the mist, and a horn sounded.

"We're in trouble now," he said. "Here they come."

"I see them," Garth replied. "Do we stand or run?"

"They're three to our one," Will said without slacking pace. "Too many of them for us to fight, especially out here in the open ground. We'll have to run for it."

"That's no good either," Seamus cut in. "Their mounts are fresher than ours. We should have taken some of the baron's horses while we had the chance."

"I'd just as soon not add horse thievery to our list of crimes," said Garth.

"If I'd thought of it in time, I would have," Will said. "It wasn't *your* gallows they were building in the courtyard."

He glanced back over his shoulder again. So far the riders coming from Harrowholt had not succeeded in shortening the gap, but he knew it was only a matter of time. "We'll head for the river," he said. "Duke Anlac's law doesn't stretch to the other side. Once we cross the bridge, we'll be safe."

Tostig snorted. "Much you know about the way a lord's men chase outlaws," he said. "If they catch us on the other shore, they'll drag us back to Harrowholt—or just kill us on the spot. They'll settle things later with the king in Orwick, if he ever finds out."

"I know," said Will. "But Nordanglia's our best hope just the same. If they overtake us, I'll turn and fight. The rest of you keep on going."

Seamus made a rude noise. "With all respect, my lord, I didn't pull you out of Baron Henry's strong room to leave you behind at the border."

"The squire's right," said Garth. "You don't get rid of us that easily."

Will felt a surge of affection for his friends. The warmth of it went a long way toward offsetting the pain of Duke Anlac's betrayal. "Then let's ride."

The sun was full up and the mist was gone by the time they reached the bridge. The knights from Harrowholt still pursued them, not drawing any closer, but not falling back. Will had long since given up hope that the knights would abandon the chase at the border. Baron Edric was the duke's man, after all; the lord of Grimmersfell wasn't going to raise a protest about Suthanglian knights chasing a malefactor across his lands.

All they have to do is keep us in sight until our horses give out, Will thought, *and then they'll have us.*

It wouldn't be long, either. Grey Gyfre was a gallant steed, but almost played out after the long ride; Will's friends had ridden almost as fast and far the day before, when they came north with Duke Anlac and his retinue.

"Somebody lend me a sword," said Will. "It's going to come to a fight soon, I think."

Then he shaded his eyes with his hand and looked at the road ahead. "Or maybe not just yet. We're getting near the edge of the forest. If we go in there, we may have a chance to hide out long enough for our horses to rest."

"Unchancy things happen in the forest," said Tostig. When Will didn't disagree, he went on, "But you're right about it being our only hope. My father always says that once an outlaw's gone to ground in the woods, it's pure luck if you can catch him after that."

"That had better be the truth," said Will. "Because we're outlaws, right enough."

He turned Grey Gyfre away from the high road to Orwick and toward the shelter of the trees. His companions followed. Looking back, Will saw that the riders from Harrowholt must have guessed what he intended, because they increased their pace for the first time since the chase had begun.

Will urged Gyfre to greater speed, but he knew the effort was futile. Slowly but steadily the pursuers narrowed the gap. By the time Will and his friends reached the edge of the woods, the duke's men were barely a spear's cast behind them.

"Scatter, everyone!" Will cried. "It's your only chance. For the love of God, Seamus, lend me your sword and go!"

Seamus brought his horse closer, but whether to obey the command or to stay and fight Will never learned. A tremendous crashing noise sounded in the underbrush ahead of them, as of something very heavy moving very fast. Once again, as in the great hall of Harrowholt the night before, Will felt time folding around him, so that for an instant he was back in the woods near Restonbury, riding out with his friends on the day before his knighting.

But these woods held the deep-shadowed green of summer, not the near-golden shimmer of early spring; he was the quarry now, and not the hunter. And what came charging at speed from the depths of the forest was no deer, but a wild boar of tremendous proportions: red-eyed, big as a boulder, its scarred head and flanks a dirty, pallid white.

"Run!" Will shouted, pulling Gyfre out of the way of the boar's headlong rush. Not even the duke's men on the trail behind them were as much of a threat, at this moment, as the maddened beast. He heard Garth shouting and Seamus cursing in Iernish. But the charging boar paid no heed to any of them; it ran through the center of their group without stopping and continued onward in the direction of Duke Anlac's knights.

Will seized the opportunity and urged Gyfre deeper into the forest. Driven by fear, the grey palfrey responded with a burst of unexpected speed, and the other horses were close behind. Soon they were a long way from the edge of the woods, and the sounds of pursuit no longer filled the air behind them. Will slowed the spent Gyfre to a walk, dismounted, and glanced about.

"I think we've gotten away," he called to the others. "You were right, Tostig, the forest did it for us—now all we have to do is find our way out again."

Tostig pointed. "We could ask him, I suppose."

Will looked through the trees in the direction of the squire's gesture. He saw where the growth thinned to make a natural clearing. A campfire in the center of the clearing had burned down almost to ashes. Beside the smoldering campfire slept a man in armor, wrapped up in a familiar woolen cloak.

The hair on the back of Will's neck rose, and the skin prickled all down his spine.

"Yes," he said, through dry lips. "You all stay here. I'll go see."

He handed Gyfre's reins to Seamus and started forward. When he reached the sleeping man, he looked down and saw his fears confirmed. The sleeper was himself.

I know where we are now, he thought. *And I know when.*

He frowned. Once again magic had reached into his life unasked—this time throwing his pursuers into disarray and then somehow leading him backward three days or more to this clearing in the forest.

I suppose I should be glad something doesn't want me to die on a gallows in Harrowholt's courtyard, he thought. *But I can't help wondering what it does want me for . . .*

He glanced down again at his other self. The knight who slept there on the mossy ground looked much younger than Will felt, and his beardless face was unmarked except for a line of worry between the brows that not even slumber had erased. The sleeper's black wool cloak fell away a little from his body to reveal the hilt and scabbard of a sword.

Will recognized Duke Anlac's gift—the sword that had been taken from him while he slept. *I was never meant to give it over in disgrace,* he realized. *And whatever has brought me here wants me to have it back again.*

He stooped down to withdraw the blade from its scabbard and then hesitated. *If I take the sword this time, what else am I taking with it . . . and from whom?*

It didn't matter. The sword was his. He had picked it up willingly when he knew it would bring him nothing but death, and he would pick it up now. Gently, so as not to waken the sleeper, he drew the blade from its scabbard. Then he straightened and backed away, not daring to turn around until he had reached the shelter of the trees.

"Why didn't you wake him?" Garth asked after Will had rejoined his friends.

"I was afraid of what might happen," said Will. "I . . . knew him, you see."

Garth looked at the sword Will carried in his right hand, and his eyes widened slightly in recognition. "I understand" was all he said.

"Where do we go now?" asked Tostig. "All this country is new to me."

"We're somewhere west of the high road and south of Orwick," Will said. "That much I do know. So if we ride north and east we'll be heading in the direction we want to go."

One day passed, and another, before they came out of the deepest woods onto the high road again. By that time they were considerably farther north than Will had expected. The land here was open and rolling, and mountains had appeared on the horizon to the west, like a hanging bank of blue clouds.

Seamus waved a hand in the direction of the distant highlands. "My home's beyond those and over the sea," he said. "A long way to go home, with nothing in my pockets besides wood-shavings and lint. So I suppose it's off to Orwick for me with the rest of you, and swear fealty to King Morcar—if he'll take it from outlaws and oathbreakers like us."

Garth swung around in his saddle. "Hold your tongue if you can't speak the truth," he said. "I haven't broken any oaths, and neither has anyone else here."

"You know that and I know that," said the squire. "But the world knows only what Duke Anlac and Henry of Harrowholt have decided to tell—and who can say what stories that precious pair may have concocted about us by now?"

"Speak respectfully of your superiors, at least," Garth told him. "Whatever they may have done."

Seamus flushed red between his freckles. "Superiors, is it?" he said. "My family's as good as anyone's, and better than some. My mother's grandfather was a king in Ierne."

Will sighed. "Garth, Seamus . . . please. We're tired and we're hungry. Let's not make it worse by quarreling."

The knight and the squire fell silent again. And in the quiet, far away behind them, Will heard the rising two-note call of a hunting horn.

They looked at one another. Tostig was the first to speak. "Maybe some lord is out after deer," he said. "Or a shepherd is calling the sheep into the fold."

"Maybe," said Garth. "But probably not. Shepherds in these parts use dogs and whistles, and I haven't seen any sign of deer these last two days."

"Whoever it is," Seamus said, "I want to be far away before he gets here."

"Then we'll never know who's following us," Will said.

Tostig gave a short laugh. "Let me show you an outlaws' trick my father told me about," he said. "We can leave the high road and circle back to our own trail, where we can find a good place to hide out and see who comes along after us."

"Your father knows more outlaws' tricks than the outlaws do," said Will. "It's a good thing for the shire that he works at keeping the King's Peace instead of breaking it."

By midafternoon they had retraced their way to a point about a mile beyond where they had left the forest. Tostig halted them at a low, brush-covered hill overlooking the road.

"Now we lie quiet and wait," he said. "Either those folks with the horn come along after us, or they don't."

Will nodded. "We can stay here tonight, and if nothing happens we'll move out tomorrow at first light. There's no sense blundering around in the dark."

The afternoon wore on. Dusk settled over the hills, sunset flaring over the highlands to the west. Will had just awakened from a long nap to take his turn at the guard when he heard the sound of horses approaching. He prodded the other members of the party with his foot to alert them as well. Then he and Garth crawled forward to lie belly-down amid the roots and brambles of the bushes, where they could watch the road and whoever might come along it.

They didn't have to wait for long. Out of the deep woods rode a mounted band, with tall spears upraised and banners flying. At their head on a white horse rode a damsel clad in a coat of mail, with her long brown hair flowing loose and uncovered. Will looked at her face and felt his heart grow cold as a clot of earth between his ribs, for her face was the face of Isobel of Harrowholt. Beside her on a black horse rode a spurred and belted close-helmed knight. The green shield he carried bore the picture of a leaping silver stag.

At the back of the pair rode a thick press of armored knights—Ohtere, Beorn of Stanburh, and others whom Will did not know. *So many*, thought Will, shuddering. *So many.*

One of the host of silent riders turned his head as he passed the bushes where the Restonbury knights lay hidden. He didn't have a face: only a bleached skull, the empty eye sockets gaping darkly beneath the helmet's rim.

Will looked over at Garth. From the expression on his face, he had seen the same thing.

At that moment the damsel in armor lifted a curved horn to her lips and blew a high, wavering note. The band of dead men and their leader spurred forward at the sound, heading north up the high road.

For a long time after the riders had gone out of sight, Will and Garth lay among the bushes without speaking. It was almost full dark before Garth finally pushed himself upright.

"Where have you been, Will Odosson," he said quietly, "and what have you done, that Lord Death and his lady are riding on your trail?"

Will swallowed hard. "I don't know," he said. "But I'm not staying here to meet them before my time."

Garth shook his head soberly. "Maybe this *is* your time. And our time, too."

Will looked at his friend. Garth was pale and set-faced. The sight of the grisly cavalcade had struck hard at him.

"Do you regret following me, then?" Will asked. The bitter note in his own voice startled him. Duke Anlac's ill usage had left a deeper mark than he'd thought. He might still trust in his friends, but the trust was no longer easy and unthinking.

Garth didn't seem to notice the bitterness. "No regrets," he said. "Whatever happens will happen. You're right, though; we shouldn't stay here where anyone can follow our trail and come on us from behind."

Will and Garth made their way back down the hill and joined the squires. Neither one said anything about what they had seen. They all mounted their horses, then crossed the road and pressed on westward while the last colors of the sunset purpled into the gloaming of summer. To the north, along the road to Orwick, the hunting horn sounded again.

chapter
13

Three days later Will and his companions were still riding—though they weren't any closer to Orwick, in Will's estimation, than they'd been when the chase began. This day they had traveled since sunup through open land that grew steeper as they rode. And, as it had done again and again during their journey, the call of a hunting horn sounded at intervals from the hills behind them to the south and east.

Seamus scowled. "I wish they'd stop that, whoever they are," he said. "Or else close in and get it over with."

Will thought about Lord Death and his consort, with their retinue of ghostly knights, and shook his head. "Don't wish that," he said. "What's happening is bad enough. We're being pushed north and west, farther and farther away from Orwick."

The squire looked curious. "Why, I wonder?"

"I'm not sure I want to know," Garth said. "There's already too much magic in this for my comfort."

"I'm with you on that," said Tostig. "Magic is for wizards, not for the likes of us."

The hunting horn sounded again, its haunting notes clear and lingering in the still air. In spite of himself Will glanced back over his shoulder, even though he knew he'd see nothing but the same blank, unpeopled moorland they'd been riding through all day. For a breath or two, looking at the empty landscape, he felt like echoing Seamus—*Show yourself; make your purpose known; I'm sick of being herded about.*

Then he sighed, aware that his wishes held no great significance for anyone except himself. "We've sat here gawking long enough," he said aloud. "Let's move on."

He urged Gyfre forward. The others followed, riding on toward the higher hills that rose up in the west. Nordanglia had the name of a wilder and more desolate land than the southern kingdom, and from the time they had crossed the border north of Harrowholt until now, they had encountered no signs of any human habitation. But this evening, as the sun went down, they spied a farmstead nestled into the side of a hill.

Will looked at the snug little croft—the stone cottage with its roof of green turf, its kitchen garden, its cluster of outbuildings—and felt his spirits rising. The folk of a prosperous but isolated smallholding like this one might be glad to exchange a night's hospitality for news of the greater world.

"Let's head over that way," Will said to Garth. "We've lived on burnt oatcakes and snared rabbit for a sennight, and I'm ready to sing for my supper like a minstrel if I have to."

Garth closed his eyes and shuddered broadly. Seamus, riding close behind them, laughed outright.

"Stick to telling stories and spreading gossip," the squire advised Will. "Leave music to people who can carry a tune without the notes running out between their fingers."

"Amen to that," said Garth and Tostig at the same instant, and they all laughed. With their hearts lifted up by the prospect of warm food and good company, they rode across the rolling landscape toward the small croft.

But as they drew nearer, they fell silent again. The cottage and its outbuildings were too quiet, too empty. There were no goats or chickens in the yard, no cattle lowing in the byre, no people.

Will felt his skin prickling, and Grey Gyfre shuddered beneath him with unease.

Garth plainly felt it, too. Will saw that his shoulders were braced as if he expected a blow to fall on them, and he had already drawn his sword.

"I don't know about this place," he muttered, when Will glanced his way. "It looks all wrong."

"I don't like it either," Will said. "But there's four of us here, and if there's been trouble maybe we can help. Let's get a better look and be ready to fight if we have to."

They rode into the farmyard. This close to the cottage, Will saw that part of the roof had fallen in. All the timbers were charred, with black stains marking the stones around the windows and the doorframe. The acrid smell of burnt wood mixed with other smells that lay heavily on the still air: the stink of blood and rotting meat, and something else that Will couldn't put a name to—except to remember, for some reason, the dead troll back at the Giants' Bridge, and how its blood had fouled the water as it fought against the swords and ropes.

He looked over at the two squires. Tostig was swallowing hard, and Seamus had gone paler than bleached linen in between his freckles.

"Something bad has happened here," said Seamus tightly. "Nothing good ever smelled like this."

Tostig nodded without opening his mouth. Even Garth showed no eagerness to continue forward. Will didn't blame him; he wanted to turn Gyfre and run away himself.

"Just the same," he said aloud, "we have to look inside. Somebody might still be alive in there."

He dismounted and handed Gyfre's reins to Seamus. A moment or so later, Garth did likewise, and then Tostig. The redheaded squire took the ax that hung from his saddle, the same weapon that had killed the troll at the Giants' Bridge, and joined the knights as they advanced with drawn swords on the door of the burnt cottage.

The smell became worse as they drew nearer, until it was almost unbearable. Inside, it filled the stone walls like a solid thing: rank and thick, and full of buzzing flies. The crofter and his wife—one of the bodies still wore the bloodied scraps of a dress—lay on the packed-earth floor. Something had torn the bodies limb from limb and devoured the meat off the bones.

"They must have tried to drive it away with fire," said Tostig hoarsely. "But it didn't work."

Will turned his face away. His mouth was full of a metallic taste, like licking a knife blade. "Drive away . . . what?"

Garth shook his head. "I don't know. Like Seamus said, something bad. And hungry."

In silence they dug a shallow grave in the farmyard and buried what remained of the two corpses. Then they remounted their horses and rode on westward until the last of the twilight had gone from the sky and the stars came out. When they could go no farther, they made a rough camp on the flank of a long hill. Tostig baked oatcakes on a flat stone for supper, but nobody was able to eat more than a few bites. After a while they gave up trying.

Nobody seemed eager to go to sleep, either. Garth sat by the fire sharpening his sword as he had every night since leaving the forest. From time to time he frowned at Seamus and Tostig, who had scratched a gaming board into the dirt and were playing at nine-men's morris, using pebbles and twigs for the counters. Hunched over their game with grim concentration, the two squires didn't speak.

Meanwhile Will sat a little away from the others, pulling up blades of grass one at a time—each blade breaking away with a faint but distinct popping sound—and feeding them to the flames. His mind kept going back to that little stone farmhouse. The crofter and his wife hadn't expected whatever it was that came upon them and destroyed their comfortable existence. Yet they were dead now—dead and devoured.

Next to them, I'm the lucky one. I think.

He bit his lip. Not quite a week ago, as he reckoned time, he'd been locked in the strong room at Harrowholt, waiting for the carpenters to finish building a gallows. Now he was free and well out of Duke Anlac's reach; but that escape had brought him into the realm of something that he couldn't identify and didn't understand, except that it seemed to be pushing him onward toward an unknown fate.

He didn't even mind that so much anymore—*if the duke had hanged me,* he thought with bitter humor, *I suppose I wouldn't mind that by now, either*—but he didn't like the prospect of watching his particular wyrd entrap his friends as well, when their only crime had been loyalty to him.

If I thought I could convince them to turn back and let me go on alone—

The barely formed idea dissipated like woodsmoke before Will could finish it. He came back to the present with a jerk. He had caught the sound of footsteps approaching from the bottom of the hill.

The image of the dead crofter and his wife rose up in his mind, and the sound of Garth's voice in the burnt cottage: *"Something bad . . . and hungry."*

He put out a hand to quiet the steely, rhythmic whisper of Garth's whetstone. Garth halted the motion and sat still. In the greater silence, they heard the footsteps again—not one set, as Will had thought before, but several.

By now the two squires were also aware of the noise. Seamus

had a sword ready, and Tostig had picked up his double-bladed ax. The footsteps came closer, slowed, and stopped. Will swallowed, trying to moisten a throat gone suddenly dry.

"Who goes there?" he called out into the darkness.

Relief flooded through him when a man's voice answered, speaking plain Anglisc in the northern manner. "Alfric Ealdorman, my lord. From Caermaris-on-Sea. We're unarmed."

"Come on up to the fire, then," Will said. "And tell us what brings you out into the night unprotected."

Slowly and hesitantly a group of peasants came forward out of the shadows—five of them, three men and two women, their clothing worn and earth-stained, their faces gaunt and shadowed with hunger and exhaustion. *They look like they've been on the run even longer than we have,* thought Will. *But they can't be fugitives, or they wouldn't have come anywhere near a knights' camp in the first place.*

"You're a long way from home," Garth said to them. He wasn't smiling, and he hadn't put away his sword. "What are you looking for on this side of the mountains?"

A stocky man with a square jaw and thick pepper-and-salt hair took a step forward and went down on one knee in front of Will. "We're seeking for help in our time of need, my lord," he said, as if Garth had not spoken. His voice marked him as the one who had named himself Alfric Ealdorman. "We've sworn to walk all the way to Orwick, if need be, and beseech the king to send us a champion."

Will took a longer look at the peasants: no half-starved plowmen and shepherds, here, but folk who had once been prosperous. From the style of Alfric's garb, Will suspected that he had been Caermaris-on-Sea's miller and a leading man in his village.

"What about your own lord?" Will asked him. "He should either champion you himself or provide someone who will."

Alfric shook his head. "He can't do either one of those things, sir knight. He's dead."

"Dead?" Will rocked back a little, startled. "What happened?"

"An ogre," said the older of the two women. "People say it came across the Giants' Causeway from Ierne when the tide was low. It's a man-eater—gone from killing and eating our sheep to killing and eating our shepherds."

"And our priest," Alfric said. "The ogre ate him and left his bones on the church steps next morning out of spite."

"Didn't your lord have a wizard?" Garth asked.

"He did," said a third villager. "The ogre ate him, too. Broke into his tower one night while he was casting spells, went straight across the border of a magic circle that was supposed to keep out everything on earth and demons, too, and snapped his neck before he could finish chanting."

"After that," concluded Alfric, "everybody ran away, and we resolved to tell the king in Orwick about our plight."

"I see," Will said. He felt a chill suspicion forming at the edges of his mind, like the rim of ice that grows around a basin of water on a cold winter night. "And so you've been traveling eastward . . . how long?"

"A week, sir knight."

The suspicion solidified into certainty. Will glanced over at Garth and the others and saw the same awareness mirrored in their faces.

A week ago some unknown magic broke in and saved us from the duke's riders. And—something—has been herding us north and westward ever since.

For this?

They'd all seen the desolation back at the farm. They had an understanding, better than any words could have given them, of what an ogre could do. But Garth wasn't going to say anything, Will could see that already, and neither were Seamus and Tostig.

Will shuddered. *That leaves it in your hands, Will Odosson. You can let Alfric and his friends go on to Orwick, and maybe King Morcar has a spare champion to lend them, and maybe he doesn't. Or you can give up and do what the magic wants: Go to Caermaris-on-Sea and kill the ogre yourself.*

Or die trying.

As soon as the thought came to him, he knew it was the truth. It settled easily into the framework of Master Finn's prophecy, like a gem into its setting. He was outcast, all but outlawed, and his own overlord had disowned him. He owed no service to any man, and no obligations remained to bind him except his own word and the vows of knighthood, to protect the helpless and aid the weak.

"Now that you are a knight, your word is all you are."

Even Duke Anlac had trusted him to speak the truth. What other reason could Anlac have had for wanting to hang him before he could say anything at all?

All this went through Will's mind in the space of a few heartbeats, while he sat looking into the square, earnest face of Alfric Ealdorman. But in the end he could only think of one thing: that a man could grow mortally weary of waiting on the conclusion of a prophecy.

"I'll fight the ogre for you," he said to the villagers. "I'm not one of the great champions, but I'm a lot closer than Orwick. If I fail, you can always try the king afterward."

"Have you gone mad?" Garth demanded, in the same instant as Tostig said, "You saw what happened to those crofters. Do you want to end up like that?"

Seamus, who had turned bright red while Will was talking, pushed himself to his feet and caught Will by the arm. He spoke in a hoarse, angry whisper. "Are you telling me I pulled you out of Baron Henry's strong room—and killed a man doing it—just so you could throw your life away?"

Will shook his head at Garth and Tostig and held out a placating hand toward his squire. "No, Seamus. I think you saved me from the hangman so that I could help these people when they needed me."

"But why you?" Garth asked. "Alfric had the right idea—go to Orwick and ask for a champion."

"It's a long way to Orwick," Will said. "And I'm here already. Besides, you know as well as I do that there's magic at work. It's been pushing me toward this ever since we left Harrowholt."

Garth just looked at him. "Right. And we saw what kind of magic it was, too."

"I'm not asking anybody to come with me," said Will. "Go back home if you like, or go to Orwick and keep Alfric and his people company on the road."

"No," said Tostig. "I've come this far with you, and I'm not turning back now. One man against an ogre is too narrow a chance."

"Two's not much better," Seamus said. "Make it three."

"You can't—," Will began.

"They have already," Garth told him. "Make it all four of us. That way some of us have a chance of coming back alive."

chapter 14

When full light came the knights and squires started out for Caermaris-on-Sea. Alfric Ealdorman had told them the way and had offered to go with them as a guide, but Will told him to go on to Orwick with the other villagers.

"If the road's as clear as you say, we can find it unguided," he said to the miller. "And you shouldn't waste any more time on us. Make haste to Orwick and petition King Morcar to send his champion in case we fail."

They parted then—the villagers heading eastward, while Will and his friends continued on. The road westward led through a narrow gap in the hills, where steep, rocky slopes rose up out of banks of green pine trees on either side. The highland air had a fresh, resinous tang, and the clear yellow sunlight that shone down into the gap touched the edges of everything with a hint of gold.

In spite of all that had happened, Will felt his spirits lifting as he rode. For the first time in weeks he was following a course he had chosen for himself, free of the tangle of lies and political advantage that had ensnared him on the border. Maybe the choice would be the end of him, as Master Finn had predicted, but at least it would be an honorable end.

And I've seen enough by now that weren't, he thought. *Hywel and Osbert, Ohtere, even poor Beorn . . . No, it's better like this.*

The journey through the mountains took almost a week. On the seventh day after they had met the villagers from Caermaris-on-Sea, the trail began to tend generally downward. Not long afterward, the sound of rushing water came from among a jumble of rocks off to the travelers' left.

Will smiled. If Alfric Ealdorman had spoken truly, they would reach the ogre's main hunting grounds before nightfall.

Seamus rode up beside him. "You're too cheerful about this," the squire said in a low voice. "Have you made up your mind to die? Is it because of what the duke did to you back at Harrowholt?"

"I'm not worried about that anymore."

"That's what I mean," Seamus told him. "You *ought* to be worried about it. *I* would be."

Will laughed under his breath. "The ogre doesn't care if I'm a duke's liege man or not. So why should I?"

They rode on, following the course of the stream, and emerged from the hills near the end of the day. In the distance ahead of them they saw a sheet of open water that shone like burnished metal all the way out to the western horizon.

"What lake is that?" Tostig asked.

"That's no lake; it's the sea," Seamus told him. "Just like at Harrowholt, only on the other side. Sail west from here and you'll reach Ierne."

A castle stood on a crag overlooking the water. Before long the mountain trail Will and his friends were following became a road that ran past the castle and down to the village at the ocean's edge. As soon as they came within earshot of the castle, Will nodded to Seamus. The squire put his cupped hands to his mouth and hailed the walls.

"Hello the castle!"

No response came, not even a challenge. Will glanced up at the walls, where sentries ought to be making their rounds from point to point, and saw nothing—only the banners snapping in the wind that blew off the western sea. Caermaris Castle was nothing but an empty shell.

"No help there," said Garth.

Will shook his head. "If there were, we wouldn't be here."

They left the castle behind and rode on downhill into town, a small place but clearly once a prosperous one. Houses of wood and stone stood close together along the main thoroughfares: the road from the castle and a second road that ran along the edge of the water. A church stood where the two roads met. Everything was silent: no barking dogs, no clucking and cackling chickens, none of the crying and shouting and chattering of people who live and work in close quarters. The golden light of late afternoon shone down on streets as shadowed and empty as the rest of the ogre's hunting ground.

"Nobody's here," said Will. "Alfric Ealdorman told the truth. They've all gone."

"Then what's that?"

Will looked where Tostig was pointing—at Caermaris's market cross, standing in the open square opposite the church. A woman in a blue-and-yellow dress was chained to the carved stone cross. She hung limp from the chains, sagging forward.

Garth's mouth twisted. "Somebody didn't bother to wait for a champion from Orwick. She's bait."

"Not while we're here," Will said. He swung down from Gyfre's saddle and crossed the market square in a half-dozen strides. "Find the blacksmith's shop," he called back over his shoulder. "Get me a hammer and a chisel."

When he reached the stone cross he saw that the woman was in fact a girl no older than he was. Her pale hair hung down loose on either side of her face, and her eyes were closed, as though fear or exhaustion had driven her into a swoon.

Seamus came running with blacksmith's tools. Carefully Will and the squire began to work on freeing the girl from her bonds, while Garth and Tostig rode swords-out through the rest of the town.

Whoever had chained up the young woman had used strong rivets. It took Will and Seamus working together to break open the manacles without cutting into her flesh. When the last of the iron bands fell away, she folded in the middle and toppled forward. Will caught her and eased her down onto the cobblestones, noting as he did so her dry mouth and pale skin, and the purple shadows underneath her closed eyes.

"Water," he said. "She needs water."

Seamus ran back to the horses and returned with the leather bottle he carried on his saddle. Will took it and trickled water in between the girl's lips a few drops at a time.

"Who is she?" Seamus asked. "Those clothes are too fine and her hands are too soft for her to be a farm girl or somebody's maidservant."

"We can ask her soon enough. Look, she's waking up."

The girl stirred, and her eyelids fluttered open. The eyes beneath were brown, in striking contrast to her pale skin and yellow hair. She looked from Will to Seamus and back again.

"Who are you? Is the ogre dead?"

Will shook his head. "No. But we've come to kill it."

"Who are you?" she asked again.

"Will Odosson of Restonbury," he said. "A knight-errant from

Suthanglia, with my friends. Alfric Ealdorman told us about the ogre."

The girl pushed herself up into a sitting position. "But did he tell you that the ogre will not die?"

Behind Will, Seamus drew in a sharp breath through his teeth. Will glanced over his shoulder at the squire and saw that he had turned pale under his freckles. Will felt almost as pale as Seamus looked.

"We hadn't heard about that part," he said. "What do you mean—the ogre won't die?"

"People have tried to kill him," said the girl. "They always fail. Ordinary sword strokes slide off him like water drops, and even mortal blows will not stop him. I've seen him be run through with a blade and still go on to tear the face off the man who had struck him."

"Here in this town?" Will asked.

"Yes," she said. "It was the lord of Caermaris Castle who struck the blow I told you of, when the ogre killed our priest and threw his bones onto the church steps. After the ogre killed the lord's wizard, too, Alfric Ealdorman and Hulda Brewestere said it was time to ask the king in Orwick for help because there was none left here for us. After they had gone most of the people ran away into the hills, but a few stayed behind for one more try at killing the ogre before they fled."

Will looked at the girl's wrists. Scrape marks and bruises marked her pale skin where the manacles had rubbed against it. "How did you come to be chained like that?"

"They needed someone to act as the bait," she said, "to keep the ogre from tracking down the ones who fled, and draw him into range of the archers. We all drew lots, and I lost."

Will was about to ask her what had become of the archers when Garth and Tostig came riding back. They looked pale and unhappy. Garth, at least, had come in time to hear the girl's last words.

"You can forget about those archers," he said. "Your ogre got to them first."

"He knocked open their skulls," Tostig added. He'd managed to keep his voice steady, but his eyes were wide and dark, almost all pupil. "And ate their brains out."

Far back in the highlands a horn blew, distant and wavering, as if to underscore his words. Will heard the sound; it made him feel sick, almost dizzy—but not with the fear he'd been keeping at arm's length ever since the farmhouse on the other side of the mountains. That fear was a familiar and accustomed thing, nothing more than a small part of the larger fear he'd lived with ever since Restonbury. It was like an old friend compared to the unexpected rush of anger that filled him now, welling up with such force that it nearly unbalanced him where he knelt on the cobblestones.

Fool! he raged at himself, clenching his fists to keep from screaming it aloud. *Blind, arrogant fool—working so hard at resigning yourself to death that you end up half in love with it! You told yourself that Lord Death was driving you toward this place, but you lied—you were chasing him every step of the way.*

So now you've come to your meeting, and you've brought all your friends with you. You'll have a lot to answer for, Will Odosson, when the time comes for judgment.

He closed his eyes for a moment, forcing the anger down, and made himself ask in a level voice, "Are the marks fresh?"

Garth answered, "Fresh within the hour."

Will opened his eyes again and stood up. He drew a deep breath. "Then let's track him to his lair. Here between the houses our horses aren't much good—out in the open, mounted, we'll have the advantage."

Will and Seamus mounted their horses, and Will bent down and helped the girl up onto the saddle before him. "Come along," he said. "It's not that safe where we're going, but it's safer than staying here alone."

She made no protest and rode with him in silence as the knights and squires headed down the harborside street toward the edge of town. They hadn't gone far before Garth pointed at a muddy, rubbish-strewn alley—not even a street, only a strip of ground between houses, too narrow for carts or wagons.

"The trail leads that way," he said.

"You're the huntsman among us," Will said. "Should we follow it?"

Garth frowned. "I don't like the darkness back in there. But look at the sky to the west—there's a storm coming tonight. If we lose the trail now, the rain could wash out the tracks. It might be days before we pick up the trail again."

And every day gives the ogre more chances to kill us all. "All right," Will said. "We follow it now."

With Garth in the lead, they rode single file into the depths of the alley, where the overhanging second stories of the facing houses nearly blocked the sky. Then the street took a bend, and all at once the ogre was upon them, leaping out from between two houses, tackling Seamus's horse and bringing both horse and rider to the ground.

In that first instant, all Will could think was, dazedly, *I never expected it to be so big.*

Huge, horrible—taller than a man and broader, covered all over in thick oily fur like the troll they'd slain back at the Samsach River, but with an awful, malicious intelligence in its deep-set yellow eyes—the ogre loomed in the dark alley like something from the old days when giants lived in Anglia.

It would take *a giant to kill something like this,* Will thought in desperation. But they had to fight it now, on ground of the beast's own choosing. Seamus's fallen horse blocked the alley, so that those before couldn't turn back, and those behind couldn't go forward. Seamus himself lay half under his fallen mount, pinned by its weight.

Will swung down to fight on foot. "Run if you can!" he shouted at the girl, and then turned back to the fight.

Garth had already dismounted, and his sword was dark with blood. More blood oozed thick and purplish red from the ogre's wounds, but the creature stood astride the narrow alley like a mountain of flesh and bone. Tostig was still on horseback, pressing closer and swinging downward with his ax.

The heavy blade cut into the ogre's shoulder, but even then the creature did not go down. It turned, ripping the ax from Tostig's hands, and backhanded him out of the saddle into the wall of the house behind. He hit the wall and slid downward, gasping with the force of the blow.

Will gripped his sword in both hands. "Ogre!" he shouted to distract the creature from following up the attack. "If you want an enemy, come to me!"

The ogre roared—*no*, Will realized in shock, remembering how Seamus had said the ogre in Ierne taunted its captors in human speech, *it's not roaring, it's laughing at us*—and turned toward the sound of Will's voice. Will stepped forward to add the power of his legs to the strength of his arms and shoulders as he brought his sword around in a great, looping swing that struck the ogre just below the ribs. The blade sank in deep, all the way to the creature's spine; Will felt the sword shiver when it struck bone, and his hands stung with the force of the blow.

The ogre crumbled forward like a tree cut nearly through by the forester's ax. Will yanked the sword free and chopped down into the back of the ogre's neck. Blood spurted upward, and the head rolled away to lie face down in the mire.

Will pulled himself back into a guard position and turned

slowly about. Grey Gyfre, and the girl in blue and yellow, had gotten no farther away than the alley's mouth. Everything was silent except for the panting of men and horses.

Seamus was struggling to pull himself from beneath his horse, and Tostig lay gasping for the wind that the ogre had knocked from him. Only Garth was on his feet, and he had to lean against a wall to keep upright. Will saw that the knight's left thigh had been sliced open from hip to knee by the ogre's iron-hard claws.

"How bad—?" Will asked after he could breathe again a little, and after his hands had stopped shaking.

"Men have recovered from worse," Garth replied. His voice was tight with controlled pain.

"And so will you," Will said, though the words rang hollow. He turned back to where the girl in blue and yellow sat astride Gyfre, watching them. "But at least we've killed this deathless ogre of yours, my lady."

She shook her head. "No. Look."

Will looked. The gashes in the ogre's body had grown together as it lay in the dirt. Even the mark of the killing blow across its belly had faded to nothing but a red line. Now the ogre's long arms were pulling its headless body along, crawling and scraping through the mud and slime in the direction of its severed head.

chapter 15

While they had been talking, the ogre's crawling body had almost reached its goal. The knobby, groping fingers swept back and forth in the mud until they touched the severed head. Then they tangled themselves in the thick fur and dragged the head back toward its body and shoved it roughly into place against the stub of its neck.

The raw edges of the wound closed and sealed over. The ogre's yellow eyes moved to fix Will with a baleful glare, and the slit-like pupils narrowed.

It knows I killed it, Will thought with a shiver. *And it knows how to hate. I'm not just food to it now. I'm an enemy.*

The ogre drew its feet under its body and pushed up onto hands and knees. Head drooping, it crouched for a moment as if gathering strength to rise further. Its barrel chest rose and fell with a sound like a giant bellows, enormously loud in the narrow alley. And over the ogre's labored breathing came another sound—clear, distinct, and familiar—the note of a hunting horn from the highlands beyond the town.

"Lord Death has come for more knights to join his retinue," Garth said. "He won't be denied this time, and I'm in no shape to run."

The girl spoke again, her voice low and solemn. "Is there nothing more that you can do?"

The ogre pulled itself onto its feet. Will took a long, shuddering breath and raised his sword.

"Nothing," he said. "I've run away from a wizard's prophecy long enough. Here's where it ends."

"Then it's time," said the girl. The words had a formal cadence, like an incantation or a prayer. "What's freely willed and freely given, let it be freely spent and done."

Will felt a shaking in the air, as if somewhere close at hand an immense bell was tolling with a note so deep it could not be heard, only absorbed as it washed over him and broke, wavelike, against his skin. The ogre ceased to move; its chest no longer rose and fell with its breath. Garth also, when Will turned to look at him, was wrapped in the same eerie stillness. So were the two squires and all the horses.

Carefully Will turned around and looked again at the girl, who had dismounted from Grey Gyfre to stand close behind him. She alone remained unaffected by the enchantment that had fallen over his companions; instead she seemed to fade and shift before his eyes, at one moment showing him the pale hair and haggard face of the girl he had taken down from Caermaris's market cross, and in the next moment the brown wavy tresses of Isobel of Harrowholt. Only the dark brown eyes were the same.

In between her upraised hands Isobel held a sphere of light that spun and glowed and changed colors seemingly at random.

"What have you done?" Will asked.

Isobel looked at him gravely over the glowing, spinning colors. "Time has stopped. Or slowed down until you can't see its passage; it doesn't matter which. While the enchantment holds, we stand outside of time."

"What good is that? It won't help my friends or stop the ogre—unless I can strike the creature again here and scatter the pieces so far apart that nothing can rejoin them."

"You're outside time," said Isobel, "and the ogre is within it. Any blow you struck would be always falling and never touching flesh, over and over again forever. No—there's something you have to do before the ogre can die."

"What?" Will demanded. His chest ached from the sudden flame of hope, the first real hope in days. "Tell me!"

"I'm not the one who knows," Isobel said. "Come."

She turned, still holding up the sphere, and walked out of the alley. Will glanced about once more at his friends and at the ogre, all unmoving in this timeless place, then sheathed his sword and followed after her.

"Are you really Isobel of Harrowholt," he asked as they left the dark alley for the open street, "or is this just some kind of wizard's trick?"

"I am Isobel," she said. "But not of Harrowholt any longer—no more than you're of Restonbury."

That stung. "It's better, I suppose, when it's your own idea. Why didn't you tell me you were a wizard?"

"Because I'm not," she said. "I'm only a wizard's student. And I didn't tell you because I couldn't tell anybody."

"Nobody at all?"

She looked back at him over her shoulder with a quick, rather sad smile. "You've seen for yourself how gently my father and Duke Anlac handle those who threaten their plans. I didn't dare say anything—or even go openly to join my teacher—until I'd learned enough to leave in secret and cover my own tracks. When you came early to Harrowholt, I was afraid; I thought my father meant us to marry then and there."

"So you ran."

"Yes," she said. "And found my teacher waiting for me, which I hadn't expected. She told me that you were the knight she'd come to Suthanglia to find—"

"To kill the ogre?"

Isobel frowned slightly. "I think so. She was worried about you, anyhow. She said that you were riding into trouble and that leaving you to deal with my father and Baron Edric and the duke was like throwing an honest man into a pit of vipers. She told me to practice my skills with the lesser magics by watching you and keeping you safe."

As she spoke Isobel led the way down the street that curved along the waterside. She fell silent as they neared the harbor. At first Will heard no other sound. The whole town was caught within the spell, and the unechoing silence of its empty streets made ordinary quietness seem only an imitation. But as they drew closer to the docks, the quiet was pierced by a high, sweet sound, as of voices singing without words or with words that could not be understood, like music in a dream.

"The singing," Will said. "Do you hear it?"

"Not clearly," Isobel said. "But if you can hear it, that will be good enough."

When they reached the wooden dock, Will saw that a ship lay tied up there, a long narrow vessel with a high curving prow and a single square-rigged mast. He looked at the ship uneasily, while the wordless music flowed over and around him.

When we rode into town, there weren't even any fishing boats tied up.

"That ship," he said. "Is it something outside of time as well?"

"Of course," said Isobel, without stopping or turning her head. "How else can you go where you need to be?"

"How else," repeated Will unhappily.

Nevertheless, he followed Isobel down the dock to the ship. When he looked out at the harbor, he saw that the waves had frozen in their curls, like water carved out of crystal, and the ship lay motionless, snug up beside the dock. Isobel stepped across from the dock onto the deck of the ship, and Will followed her aboard.

Like the town, the ship was silent and empty—except for the singing. The sweet, piercing voices sounded louder than ever, filling the air around him like curls of incense. He drew in the unearthly music with every breath he took, until even his bones and sinews answered, and his whole body shivered like a fiddle string under the bow.

The music pulled at him, making him think of the river current at the Giants' Bridge, trying to drag him under and carry him downstream.

"Take care!" Isobel exclaimed, and Will saw that he had crossed the deck without knowing it, so that he stood at the rail on the seaward side of the vessel.

He looked down at the water. There amid the frozen waves he saw three—

—three what? I don't know what they are. Not women, when I can see the webs between their fingers and the dark bodies coiled like shadows beneath the water.

And not fish either, when their faces are so beautiful, and their long, pale hands . . .

One of them looked him in the face and spoke his name. Her skin was a whitish green, and the long hair that floated about her in the water was the color of sea spray on the wind.

"Will Odosson," she said, in a voice like music.

"Will Odosson of Restonbury," called the second.

"Will Odosson of nowhere at all," called the third one, and laughed at him. The laughter was part of the singing, and he could feel the notes running down his bones like water. It took all the strength he had to draw a breath and answer.

"Who are you and what do you want?"

The third sea-woman looked up at Will and smiled. "We know something," she said, "and you want to know it, too." Her smile had too many teeth in it, all thin and sharp like needles.

"What is it that you know?" he asked. "Tell me."

"Too easy, too easy," the first one said. "You have to do a favor for us first."

Will took a step backward and shook his head. "I don't like making a blind bargain."

The sea-woman ran her pale, webbed fingers through the white drift of her hair and looked at him through the strands. "There is an ogre," she said, "and he will not die."

"He came over the sea from Ierne," sang the second one, "across the great stone causeway that the giants built when Anglia was young."

"And we know the ogre's thoughts," said the third. "Because he came to Anglia across the water, and we know the thoughts of all creatures that go across the water."

The three were speaking almost together now, their voices alternating and interweaving in weird, unearthly harmonies. Will felt the music twining itself like ropes around him, drawing itself tighter with every word the sea-women sang.

"The ogre thinks he is immortal, because he's hidden his death—"

"—because he's put it away where no one can find it—"

"—a wizard did that for him, to save his own life—"

"—took the ogre's death and hid it, hid it away in an egg, in a bird's egg on the seashore—"

"—the ogre killed the wizard anyway, so no one would know how to find his death—"

"—but we saw him hide it. And we know his thoughts."

The singing stopped. The sea-women looked at Will from round unblinking eyes that were even greener than the ocean. Nothing moved.

There's no time here, Will thought. *They can wait forever for an answer.*

He turned back toward Isobel. She stood as she had before, with the globe of spinning colors held up before her.

"The sea-women," he said. "Do they speak true?"

"I'm not the one who can hear them," she said. "But the daughters of the sea speak for their own reasons and not for ours."

"I understand," he said. "But I don't think I have a choice." He turned back to the sea-women floating in the water. "I'll take your bargain. Show us the way."

The sea-women made no reply, except to vanish beneath the surface of the unchanging waves. The ship began to move forward through the water. No wind blew to fill the sail, and no oars rose and fell to push away the water with their blades. The ship cut through the ocean without disturbing it, leaving not a ripple of wake behind.

The harbor and houses of Caermaris-on-Sea grew small and vanished behind them, and soon even the towers of Caermaris Castle sank below the eastern horizon. Will thought that the ship began to go even faster, but he couldn't be sure. Now that they were out of sight of land, he had nothing against which to measure their progress but the unmoving sea and the sky.

"Where are we going?" Will asked Isobel. "Do you know?"

She shook her head. "The daughters of the sea are guiding us now. We can only wait."

Will sat down on the deck and leaned back against the mast. Isobel remained standing, with the spinning globe between her hands. Will watched the changing colors—blue, red, green; then yellow, white, and blue again—until he felt himself growing sleepy. He shook his head to clear it.

"Tell me something," he said, more to keep awake than for any other reason. He didn't think it would be good to fall asleep during this voyage outside of time; if he did, he wasn't certain that he would ever wake up.

"If I can," Isobel said.

"How did you come to be chained to the market cross in Caermaris-on-Sea?"

"I told you. I was there as bait."

He looked at her. "Bait for the ogre—or bait for something else? For a knight, maybe, who could hear the sea-women singing and bargain with them for what they know?"

Isobel didn't answer for a long time, so that he almost gave up hope for a reply. But at length she said, "Do you know the difference between the lesser and the greater magics?"

"I'm not a wizard."

"Neither am I," she said. "That takes years, more years than I've been alive—but I know something of the way in which magic works. With the lesser magics, a thing happens, and magic clearly is the cause."

Will thought for a while about what she had said. "Do you mean that all this—" he flung out one hand in a gesture that included the ship, the ocean, and the whole time-frozen world "—is one of the *lesser* magics?"

"What else could it be?" she asked.

"Never mind," he said. "Go on. The greater magics."

"They also make things happen, but not so that magic appears to be the cause."

"Oh."

Isobel was looking away from him now, her attention fixed on the spinning colors between her hands.

"I spoke with a wizard once," she said, "who could work the greater magics. She told me about a time she was traveling in the south of Anglia . . . to buy a pig, as it happened, since even a wizard can have a taste for bacon . . . when she was set upon by a pair of outlaws who would have taken the pig and killed her for sport afterward. When she looked into their hearts, she saw that they were wicked men, who had done such things many times before. And so she cast a spell of death upon them."

"I see," Will said. His hands were cold and trembling; he

clasped them together and the shaking stopped. "What happened next?"

"A young knight appeared and slew them both."

He wet his lips. "She summoned him?"

"He thought he came that way by chance," said Isobel. "That's how the greater magics work. But it *was* magic, as surely as if the ground had opened up beneath the outlaws and swallowed them whole."

Will looked down at the deck. The boards were sanded clean, without spot or blemish. "I was that knight," he said without looking up. "I came to that glade by following a white deer that no one saw but me. Now I find out that I was summoned there by magic. And you are telling me . . . I *think* you are telling me . . . that magic has summoned me again to fight an ogre that will not die."

chapter 16

"Yes," said Isobel. "No ogre can be harmed by magic. It's part of their defense against the world, my teacher says. And that's why the world needs knights and heroes: to do what wizards cannot. But look—the daughters of the sea have brought you to your destination."

Will looked and saw an island ahead on the horizon, growing larger as the ship drove on toward it. A thin column of smoke rose from a mountain in the center of the island and thinned out to nothing against the clouds above. Will watched the smoke for a short time and then frowned.

The clouds aren't moving. They're frozen in time like the water and everything else.

But that smoke—it is moving.

The ship glided onward, until it rested in a bay at the side of the island, where a pebbled beach led up to the beginnings of a forest. The island itself—down to the smallest leaf and blade of grass—was as time-stilled as the waves halted in the act of breaking on the shores. Only the drifting smoke moved, rising in slow spirals from its mountain peak.

Will pushed himself away from the mast and got to his feet. He went over to the side of the ship and looked down. The unmoving water broke into ripples and eddies as the green-eyed, white-haired sea-women rose up from below.

He didn't wait for them to speak. "If you've brought me here for a reason," he said, "then tell me what I have to do."

"There is a dragon that dwells here," the sea-women replied in their singing voices. "Kill him for us, and we will give you the ogre's death." The sea-women kept on smiling at him with their mouths full of long, sharp teeth. "Remember, Will Odosson— you gave us your word."

Will wanted to cry out that it had been an unfair bargain, but he swallowed his protests. "I made a promise," he said quietly to the sea-women, "and I will keep it."

He jumped over the side of the ship. The waves gave slightly underneath his feet, like moss on the land, then bore up his weight. He walked across the springy surface of the motionless water and through the frozen surf onto the beach, pausing on the shore to look back. Isobel remained standing on the deck, the sphere of colored light still spinning between her hands. The sea-women had disappeared from sight.

He turned inland toward the column of smoke and walked for a long time, while the sun overhead remained as fixed in the sky as the sun in a painting and the leaves and branches of the forest around him never moved. At length he came to a part of the forest where the leaves were no longer green, but scorched and withered.

He drew his sword and went onward. Singed leaves gave way to bare branches and then to charred tree trunks standing on ground covered by drifted ash.

Seeing the devastation, he began to feel afraid all over again. *This is what a dragon does to the place where it lives. Killing a troll is like cleaning out vermin . . . get enough people and the right weapons, and it's easy. Killing a dragon, though . . . that's something heroes in ballads do.*

"This isn't a ballad," he said aloud. His voice was flat and echoless in the enchanted silence. "This is real."

The ashes changed to red coals, and then to fire rising from black, fallen timbers. The coals gave no heat, and the flames were steady and unmoving. In the midst of the fire was a great, coiled body covered with black and grey scales, and a massive head with a column of smoke drifting skyward from its deep red nostrils. Unlike everything else in this place, the smoke moved—puffing up in a cloud and then thinning out again as the dragon breathed.

As Will stood looking, the creature blinked one enormous amber eye and turned its head in his direction. Its mouth opened, releasing a gout of fire. The flame unrolled toward Will like a carpet being unrolled in his father's chamber at Restonbury, and almost as slowly.

He stepped aside and the flame went past him. Then the dragon shut its mouth and the flame died. The dragon blinked again, its upper eyelids lowering at the same time as the lower lids were rising. This time when its mouth opened a low, rumbling sound came forth.

It's talking, Will thought. *In ballads, the heroes always speak politely to the dragon before they fight with it.*

He cleared his throat. "Sir Dragon," he said in respectful tones, "I regret that I am here to kill you."

The dragon's mouth opened again. This time a clear alto voice came out. "Ah," the voice said, "a human creature. Who told you to kill me? Was it the sea-women?"

"Yes."

"And you chose to believe them? I tell you, the daughters of the sea are all liars."

"I've never heard that dragons are particularly truthful."

"Charming," said the worm, bringing its head forward and looking at Will out of eyes that reflected the color of the flames around him. He could see himself as well in those double mirrors—a small, unterrifying figure. Even the long sword in his hand seemed nothing to threaten such a creature. "The sea-women desire your death. They eat the flesh of drowning men and keep their souls in cages under the sea."

Will thought of the long, sharp teeth of the sea-women, and their green, inhuman eyes. He remembered their voices, high and singing as they spoke of the undying ogre. *"He came to Anglia across the water, and we know the thoughts of all creatures that go across the water."*

The dragon was probably telling the truth, he realized, but it didn't matter.

"The sea-women can tell me something I have to know," he said. "Your death is the price of their knowledge."

The dragon blinked again. "Ah . . . but will they tell you, once you have killed me?"

"I won't know until I ask them."

"If you live to ask them," the dragon said, and sprang at Will. It had moved slowly before, but it was fast enough now, and Will was so used to the frozen world that he almost didn't react in time, lifting up his sword in an attempt to ward off the crushing blow that he knew was coming.

But the blow never fell. The dragon kept on going. It leapt past him and unfurled leathery wings from its sides. The wings beat once, twice, sending ashes swirling, and then the dragon took to the air and was gone.

Will stood alone in the middle of the field of ashes for some time, feeling rather foolish. At last he sheathed his sword and started to walk back the way he had come.

On a cliff overlooking the sea, he paused to look down toward the ocean. He saw the little cove where the ship had landed, but it was empty, as was the sea, all the way out to the distant horizon—even though the sun was still frozen in the sky, and the waves remained caught in the act of breaking on the round stones of the beach.

He felt a moment of panic. *This is unjust,* he thought angrily. *I'm not a wizard. If somebody needs me to fight outlaws, or trolls, or even an ogre, I'll do my best and die if I have to. But I never asked to be snatched out of time and brought here, and then to be abandoned.*

He stood there undecided for a little while longer, then turned his back on the sea. He searched the sky overhead for any sign of the dragon and saw nothing, only the unmoving clouds like painted patterns on the sky. Then he frowned and shaded his narrowed eyes with his hand. Something *was* moving in the sky above the island's central mountain—colored lights that danced and spun like a dazzle in the air.

He remembered Isobel standing on the deck of the ship, with the globe of colored lights spinning between her hands. The distant lights above the mountain could have been the same thing, only grown large and taken far away.

I don't know if it's a sign meant to guide me, he thought, *or a trick meant to lead me astray, like faery-lanterns in the woods. But it's all I have.*

For the second time since coming to the island, he began walking inland. He couldn't tell how long he walked, since the sun didn't change its position in the sky, and the shadows on the ground never altered. But more than once he grew so weary that he halted and lay down to rest. During these times he would sleep, rolled up in his cloak and with his sword in his hand, but when he awakened he would find the sun still in the same place.

The trees grew scarcer and the ground steeper as he walked,

until he was scrambling over rocks and scarp. When he reached the top of the mountain, he found not a peak but a kind of high plateau with a lake at its center. The lake was as timeless and immobile as the sea, and above its dark blue water hovered the spinning, many-colored sphere of light.

Where now? he wondered. The light had been his guide this far, but it seemed that this far wasn't yet far enough. In this place outside of time, the water of the ocean had borne him up until he could reach the shore. *Does that mean the lake will hold me if I walk across it to touch the spinning colors?*

He shook his head. *I don't even know if anything will happen when I get there.*

"The only thing to do is try," he told himself sternly.

He set out to force a way through the brambles and vines that grew in tangled knots around the lake. When he reached the shore, he squared his shoulders and stepped out onto the water. It was soft and resilient like the ocean had been. The footprints that he left behind him flowed slowly together until no trace of his passing remained.

He thought that he'd kept his eyes on the spinning globe the whole time, but when he reached the center of the lake the globe was no longer there. He looked down. In the depths of the lake he could see the bottom, steep and rocky, sloping away to a black pit in the center of the lake from which no light returned. Then, in the center of the pit, he saw once again the dancing, many-colored lights.

As he stood there looking down, he saw that the water was rising—so slowly that he could barely see the change—up past the sides of his boots. He tried to lift first one foot, then the other, but nothing happened. He was stuck fast.

Now he did feel afraid, as he had felt afraid in the chapel at Restonbury, and in the woods near Grimmersfell when Beorn of Stanburh's ghost came to him in the dark. Even a dragon could be killed, if the one fighting it had good luck and a strong arm: Will's own great-grandfather had seen Duke Rollo kill the Great Worm of Pevensey with a single blow. But a slow drowning in this unrelenting water was something not even a hero out of legend could stop or escape.

He struggled just the same, but it didn't do any good. The water crept up past his knees and then up past his thighs. It had no wetness to it, or coldness, just a kind of horrible, thick weight. Drowning in it would be like . . . like trying to breathe in a vat of oil, or like being smothered underneath a mountain of sand.

The water reached his waist, then trapped his arms and began creeping upward to his mouth. *So this is how it ends,* Will thought as the water touched and then covered his lips. *Nothing glorious, not even anything to fight. Just dying, a long way from home.*

He fought against the temptation to open his mouth and draw the slow, remorseless water into his lungs, forcing out air and life together. *Soon enough,* he promised himself. *Soon enough. Make it work to take you. Even a small victory is better than none, if it's the last you'll ever see.*

The water closed over his head. He could hear his heartbeat pounding in his ears. The urgent rhythm slowed and steadied, until at last he realized that he hadn't drawn a breath for some time. Even more strangely, he didn't feel any need for air. He tilted his head back to look upward and saw the surface of the lake stretched out above him like a silver glass mirror.

He tried to lift his arms and found that they could move, and that he could even reach his sword—although slowly, as if instead of clear water he was moving his arm through mud or sand. How long he sank downward, supported on all sides by water that neither drowned nor chilled him, Will didn't know.

The light from the surface above him grew dimmer, until he grew tired and slept again.

If he dreamed in this strange place, he didn't remember it. When he awoke he was standing on the bottom of the lake in front of a tunnel with walls of bright gold. A light that looked like torchlight—though he couldn't see any torches—shone along the walls and sparkled off the clusters of many-colored gemstones set into the gold.

He took first one step and then another along the lake bottom, into the tunnel going toward the light. As he went his progress became easier, as if the water were thinning out until it was like air, and the light ahead of him grew stronger. Not knowing what lay ahead, and remembering the stories in the ballads about how dragons liked to live in caverns filled with gold and jewels, he drew his sword.

He rounded a bend in the passage and found himself in a chamber lit by torches and lined from floor to ceiling with tapestries and shelves of books. Seated in a high-backed chair in the center of the room was an old woman. Will looked at her. Her robes were of rich green velvet, embroidered with silver, and her wimple was of white linen under a silver circlet.

"It's about time you arrived," she said, looking sharply at Will. "And you can put up your sword."

When she spoke, Will knew where it was he had seen her before. "I hope you liked your pig," he said. He didn't move to put up his sword. "If you brought me here for a reason then tell me now, because I don't like being a wizard's plaything."

"Can you read?" the old woman asked unexpectedly.

"No," said Will, startled.

No one but priests and wizards could read. Master Finn had owned a shelf of books, back in his tower chamber at Restonbury, though not so many as the ones here. The wizard had taught Baron Odo's children something of arithmetic, and more than a little about languages—Norroenan, and Finn's native Iernish, and the Latin both the wizard and Father Padraic used every day, and Anglisc as it was spoken on either side of the border—but the books had never been opened.

The old woman was shaking her head. "There's a lack that you'll regret before your life is over," she said. "Since you can't find your answers in my books, we'll have to do this the hero's way."

"What do you mean?"

"With a game," said the old woman. "I will answer three questions for you—but only two of them honestly."

"How can I tell which ones?" Will asked.

The old woman smiled. "That's the test," she told him. "You have to decide for yourself. Use your questions wisely; weigh the answers well."

He sighed. "You've made at least one true prediction already," he said. "If I could read, I wouldn't be playing at guessing games. Why have you brought me here?"

"To be my champion in the fight against things that magic cannot touch."

Why me? Will wanted to cry out, but he saw the faint smile on the old woman's face before he opened his mouth to speak. He swallowed hard, took a deep breath, and asked instead, "How can I kill the ogre that does not die?"

He thought for a moment that the old woman looked at him approvingly. She said, "You can find his death by going to the Island of the Birds."

Just one more question, Will thought. He bit his lip in indecision. *So many things to ask: Where is this Island of the Birds? How can I get there? What am I supposed to do with the ogre's death when I find it . . . ?*

Because he couldn't possibly ask all those questions, he asked the other one instead—the one that had been haunting him

ever since the day on the trail when he had seen the helmed
rider and his array of spectral knights.

"Why does Lord Death follow me wherever I go?"

All trace of a smile left the old woman's face. "He seeks to
destroy you," she said, "before you can destroy the ogre who
does his bidding."

chapter 17

Will stared at the old woman in silence for a long moment, and his hand tightened on the grip of his sword.

He wasn't afraid, not now. He'd lived with fear so long—sometimes keeping it at arm's length, and sometimes wrapped so closely in its embrace that he could feel its chilly breath against his skin—that he didn't think words alone could frighten him anymore. He was filled, instead, with an angry conviction of the injustice of it all.

"I haven't done anything to deserve this," he said. "Out of all the knights in Anglia, why should anyone have chosen me?"

The old woman shook her head. For a moment her features changed, and she looked like the peasant woman he'd rescued from Ohtere in the woods outside Grimmersfell. Then the illusion vanished, and she looked as she had before.

"The game is over," she said. "I've answered your three questions, and it's time for you to go."

She rose to her feet. Will saw that in spite of her rich garments she was indeed as ancient as she had seemed in the woods by Restonbury—she had to push herself out of the chair with both hands gripping the carved wooden arms, and when she walked she moved stiffly, with short, careful steps.

An embroidered tapestry hung against one wall of the chamber. The old woman went over to the tapestry and pulled it aside. Behind the tapestry was a door: a heavy slab of solid oak with a black iron ring bolted onto it.

"Your way home lies through here," she told Will. "Open the door."

He stayed where he was, standing with feet planted firmly apart in the middle of the room. "Is that the truth or a lie?"

"Decide for yourself, Will Odosson. But you can't go back the way you've come, nor can you stay."

Will thought of the way he had arrived in this place. "I can see that much for myself," he said. "So forward it is."

He strode forward and pulled on the iron ring.

The door swung toward him, and in the next instant he found himself on a bright seashore where high cliffs rose above the beach to an unknown country within. He stood alone, and all was silent around him. No wind blew, and the air was neither hot nor cold. Overhead the sky was full of birds—dozens of them, hundreds of them, terns and seagulls, all fixed in their places, silent and unmoving as a tapestry pattern.

The Island of the Birds, he thought. *If the old woman spoke true, I've found the place where the ogre hid his death.*

He gazed about, but the beach where he stood was bare except for rocks and seaweed. He couldn't see any way to explore the island further except by going up the cliff. It looked steep but not sheer; he could see ledges and crevices all the way up, enough to make a path for a determined climber. Bird droppings painted long white streaks down the grey stone.

Will sheathed his sword and began the ascent. As he climbed higher, he saw that every nook and cranny in the rock face was filled with eggs. A sense of frustration welled up in him as he realized the truth. The Island of the Birds, the hiding place of the ogre's egg, was a rookery—a nesting place for hundreds, even thousands, of terns and seagulls.

Where there are hundreds, even thousands, of eggs, he thought. His weapons and his coat of mail weighed heavily on him, and he stopped to catch his breath on a ledge that was somewhat wider than the others, with enough room for a man to stand without needing to hold on. The eggs were here, as well.

Will looked down at the eggs, frowning. *Will I have to find and break every egg on this island,* he wondered, *if I'm going to destroy the one egg that holds the ogre's death?*

He picked up an egg and balanced it on the palm of his hand. The egg didn't look any different from the ones he hadn't picked up, and it didn't feel any different.

"Hundreds of eggs," he said aloud. "*Thousands* of eggs. And all of them just like this one."

He flung the egg away from him in disgust. It fell away from the cliff, growing smaller and smaller until it smashed against the stones on the beach below.

The air shivered about him—as if the sound of the egg's breaking had transformed into something that couldn't be heard at all, only felt—and time began to go forward again. The seabirds overhead began to wheel and call, the waves crashed and broke on the rocky shore, and a cold wind swept across the face of the cliff.

Then Will saw that one of the wheeling birds was far larger than the others and trailing a stream of grey smoke as it flew. *Not a bird,* he thought. The not-bird was growing bigger still as he watched it, and it wasn't changing direction at all. It was coming straight at him and moving fast.

Now Will could see the not-bird clearly and recognized it. He drew his sword and braced himself against the cliff as the dragon stooped upon him, claws extended.

He never had time to strike a blow. The beast caught him in

the talons of one scaly foot and lifted him upward in a tremendous whirl of sulfur-tinged air. The dragon carried him past the top of the cliffs to a stretch of ground dotted with grey rocks and stunted, wind-twisted trees and set him down.

In the world away from time where Will had first met the dragon, he had felt no heat in the creature's presence. Now, though, being near it was like standing next to a mountain of live coals. He began to sweat and felt the metal of his sword grow warmer in his hand.

The dragon regarded him for a moment with its enormous reptilian eyes, and then it spoke.

"Let's play a game, little hero," the dragon said. "Each one of us must answer three questions for the other and tell the truth only twice. You ask first."

Something about the dragon's cool alto voice seemed familiar now to Will. The first time he'd heard the creature talking, he hadn't noticed, but now it nagged at him. As for the game . . . that was familiar, too. The old woman in the lake had taught him the rules before she sent him to this place, though he had gotten no pleasure from learning them. Will thought hard for a moment, then phrased his first question.

"Which of these eggs contains the ogre's death?"

The dragon blinked its eyes. "I don't know."

"The sea-women saw the ogre hide his death in an egg. Do they know which egg it is?"

"Yes," said the dragon.

Good news, thought Will, *if it's the truth. All I have to do is persuade the sea-women to give up the egg. If they're telling the truth. And then I go back to Caermaris-on-Sea and try again to kill an ogre that's forgotten how to die. If I can get there at all . . .*

He moistened his lips—the heat from the dragon's body had cracked and dried them—and asked his third question. "How can I get home?"

The dragon flicked out its long, snakelike tongue in a gesture that made Will think of a human shrug. "You can't. Now it's my turn. I shall ask you three questions, and you must answer honestly twice. Do you truly desire my death?"

Will looked at the great, winged creature with his image reflected in its golden eyes, and sheathed his sword.

"No," he said.

"But you do want to go back and aid your friends?"

He thought back to the narrow alley in Caermaris-on-Sea, so far away from this rocky island. *Time is running again now, and they were all injured, maybe dying . . . what will they do when the ogre comes at them again? And where will they think I am?*

"Yes."

"Spoken like a brave and loyal knight," said the dragon, and Will couldn't tell if it was mocking him or not. "Tell me, Will Odosson—do you know who I really am?"

"No," Will replied, before he remembered that his third answer had to be untrue.

But even as he spoke he thought again about how he had played this game of questions and answers only a little while ago on the other side of an enchanted doorway. In that instant he understood why the dragon's voice should have sounded so familiar. The old woman from Restonbury and the wizard in the lake had been one person; so, too, the wizard and the dragon were one. In spite of himself he had played the game by the rules, and had answered the dragon's last question with a lie.

"Three and three," said the dragon. "You play the hero's game well, little knight."

The creature's long red tongue flicked out again and touched Will delicately on the face—too quickly for him to flinch, though afterward the mark burned like a line of fire along his cheekbone.

"You are hungry," said the dragon. "Come here. Come here to me."

Will stepped forward into the circle of heat around the dragon, where the earth was scorched and the hot air burned his lungs every time he drew breath.

"You are hungry and thirsty, Will Odosson," the dragon said again. "Here, I will give you food and drink."

The dragon lifted one jeweled claw to its chest and cut beneath one of the massive scales. A dark red liquid bubbled forth. "Here," said the dragon. "Drink."

One does not refuse the gift a dragon offers. Will stepped forward and caught the steaming sulfurous blood in his hands. He brought the red liquid to his mouth and drank it all.

The hot blood burned his lips and tongue. It raised blisters where it touched his skin, and swallowing it was like drinking fire. Over his head the dragon's wings extended as he drank, casting their shadow over him, and then swept downward. The dragon rose into the air, and the wind of its rising drove Will onto his knees and left him gasping and retching amid the ashes. By the time he had recovered, the dragon was gone.

He dragged himself to his feet and looked about. The seabirds, which had scattered and fled with the coming of the dragon, once more wheeled overhead and filled the sky with their raucous voices. The dragon's blood lay in his stomach like molten lead, and somehow its burning took the harsh cries of the birds and formed them into speech.

"Will Odosson, Will Odosson has come," the birds were calling to each other, back and forth. "Will Odosson has come, and he will destroy all of our eggs."

"No, no, no!" Will shouted back at the birds. "I don't want your eggs! I want the egg where the ogre hid his death!"

"It is not here, Will Odosson," the birds replied. Their voices were sharp and sorrowful. "It is not here."

"Then where?"

"The daughters of the sea," called the birds, "the daughters of the sea, they know, they know, where they tend their soul cages down below the brine."

I don't like this, Will thought. But his friends were fighting the ogre, and likely dying, back in Caermaris-on-Sea, and without their help he would have died a traitor's death on Duke Anlac's gallows. He sighed and started climbing down the cliff, while the seabirds circled around him and cried, "Poor Will Odosson! We shall pick his bones on the shore!"

At last he came to the strand between the cliffs and the sea. Just as on the first time he'd stood there, he saw nothing except the jagged rocks and the drifts of seaweed brought in and left by the tide. At least the sun had moved.

The sea-women eat the flesh of drowning men, Will thought. *So if I want them to come to me, I have to go to them.*

Quickly, before he could have second thoughts, he walked out into the breaking waves. The cold water beat against his chest, and then it swirled around his face. He felt the undertow snatch at his legs, and a heartbeat later the water closed over his head.

He tried to swim up to where the sweet air was waiting, but his coat of mail pulled him further into the depths, dragging him downward until his chest ached and his lungs caught fire. High, piercing voices sang in his ears, and he knew that he was drowning because the sea-women had come, with their round green eyes and their long white hair like sea spray on the wind, with their coiled bodies and their long, sharp teeth.

The singing took on words in his mind: *The dragon, what have you done with the dragon?*

He choked on the salt water, and the dragon's blood welled up in his throat, scalding his mouth and tongue all over again, choking him and burning his throat, and the singing voices cried out in delight, *He has killed the dragon and drunk its blood! We are safe, we are safe!*

The daughters of the sea took Will in their long, pale hands and pulled him lower still, down to a place below the sea where the water itself was twisted into bubbles of light—the soul cages of the sea-women. The cages glowed like pale golden lanterns, all but one. That one shone with the ugly phosphorescence of dead fish by moonlight, and Will knew that it was the ogre's egg.

He tried to pull away and swim toward it, but he was weak and the sea-women were all about him, twining their coiled bodies around his limbs and caressing his cheeks with their thin, webbed fingers. *You will drown,* their silvery voices sang in his mind, *you will drown and die and we will eat the flesh from your bones, we will keep your soul forever in the dark beneath the sea . . .*

He used the last part of his strength to seize the nearest of the sea-women and to pull his dagger from its sheath on his belt. The sea-woman only laughed inside his mind and smiled at him, baring her needle-sharp teeth. Then she twisted in his grasp and struck like a serpent for the veins in his neck.

Will brought up his knife. The point went into her throat, and dark blood floated out into the water around them. The other sea-women pulled her away. The cloud of blood in the water enveloped all of the creatures then, and the silvery voices rose in a high, hungry keening. To the daughters of the sea, all things that die in the sea are meat and drink.

Will sank down further, leaving the sea-women to their feast behind him. He knew that he was drowning. He could never swim up to the surface in his weight of chain mail, and he didn't have enough air left in his lungs to keep himself alive while he struggled to get free of the armor's weight. But while he lived, he would strive to reach the ball of green light that was the ogre's egg.

His fingers touched it. He gripped the egg hard in his left hand and drew back his dagger hand for a blow, thinking that he would use the last of his strength to break the egg and send the ogre's death out into the world.

But instead the bottom of the ocean moved and took shape underneath him as the dragon issued from beneath the sand and caught Will once again in its talons. Then Will and the dragon together rose from the seabed into the upper air in a fountain of white water.

"When I told you there was no way for you to go home," said the dragon, "I lied."

chapter 18

With great sweeps of its wings, the dragon climbed through drifts of cloud up to where the air was clear and cold. Still holding Will clutched in its talons, it flew east over the sea toward Anglia. The dark blue water sparkled far below, while behind them in the west the late afternoon sun glared like an angry red eye through banks of dark clouds.

Garth was right, Will thought unhappily. *There's going to be a storm before midnight. I'm going to have to fight the ogre after dark, in the rain.*

He couldn't speak the thought aloud—if he had tried, the wind would have whipped the words away. The turbulent air snatched and tore at him, and he clutched the ogre's egg left-handed against his chest, for fear of dropping it into the sea. The egg was larger than any bird's egg he had ever seen, almost the size of a man's head, and its mottled green-brown shell felt tough and leathery. Breaking it wouldn't be easy.

The dragon bore Will steadily eastward while the afternoon drew on toward sunset. Now that time was running again, Will feared even more for Garth and the two squires. Had they been able to defeat the ogre a second time, or had the spectral huntsman and his troop caught up with them after all?

If they're dead, then what I've done means nothing.

The dragon seemed to read his thoughts. "Whether your

friends live or die isn't yours to decide. But the ogre grows more powerful as he leaves the egg further behind—and he's already begun making forays southward across the mountains. By the time he reaches Orwick, not even all of Nordanglia's champions together will be able to stand against him. He must die here and now if he is to die at all, and you carry his death in your hands."

"But—," said Will.

The wind carried his voice away before he could finish, leaving only the thought in his mind: *But does the death I carry also mean my own?*

"Who can say?" replied the dragon, as if Will had spoken aloud. "The wizard warned you, but you took up the sword knowingly and all your wyrd follows from that. Turn aside now, and many more than you will die."

The dragon spoke no more but began circling downward. The harbor and houses of Caermaris-on-Sea came into view below, the two cross-streets and the narrow alleys, the church and the market square. The village was dim and shadowy in the last of the sunlight, except for a patch of glowing color on the wooden pier. The dragon flew toward the spot, which soon became a dark-haired girl in a blue-and-yellow dress, holding a lighted bauble in her hands.

It's stopped spinning, Will thought as the dragon released its grip and set him down at the end of the pier. *Was it the spinning that made time stand still for me?*

The dragon flapped its wings and mounted again into the evening sky, going higher and higher until it appeared no larger than the seabirds it lived among. Then it wheeled, flew westward, and was gone.

Will looked back at Isobel. The spell-globe in her hands illuminated her features—the dark hair and dark brown eyes under level brows shifting to the face she had worn in the market square. She said something Will couldn't hear, and the light from the globe flared once and died. With the colored lights gone, the magical disguise vanished completely, and she was only Baron Henry's runaway daughter in a homespun gown, looking at Will over the carved ivory bauble from the Strickland tourney.

Involuntarily Will glanced up at the sky where the dragon had vanished. "Your teacher," he said. "Is she an old woman who changes into a dragon, or a dragon who sometimes looks like an old woman?"

"I don't know," said Isobel. "Does it matter?"

Will sighed. Carefully he shifted the ogre's egg to a steadier grip and sheathed the dagger he held in his right hand. "No," he said. "I suppose it doesn't. She gave me a way to kill the ogre, and now I have to do it."

He drew his sword and started down the pier toward the town. Isobel followed without a word.

Dusk had come to Caermaris-on-Sea, and eastward above the mountains a few stars shone. The western sky was dark with clouds, with the setting sun only a sullen glow along the horizon beneath them.

Will's footsteps made almost the only sound. Isobel's lighter tread, unburdened by the weight of armor, was only a faint *slip-slipping* of leather against the stones. They made their way to the spot where Will and his friends had fought the ogre, but the now dark alley was as empty as the rest of the town.

Isobel said something in a language Will recognized as wizards' Latin. The ivory sphere lit up with a yellow glow like a lantern, illuminating the depths of the alley and the dark splotches of half-dried blood where the fight had been.

"There's a trail," she said. "Follow it."

Will glanced over at her. She was frowning, as if making the light took most of her concentration. "Can that thing stop time again?" he asked.

She didn't take her eyes away from the sphere. "No," she said. "I could only do that once."

"Oh," he said.

He bent his attention to the gruesome traces the fight had left behind. There was a lot of blood—most of it the ogre's, so deep a red that it was almost black, but the drops and streaks that led out of the alley and back toward the market cross were of a lighter color.

"Garth and the others must have killed it again," said Will to Isobel, "and gotten away while it was coming back to life."

"They can't have gone far. There's too much blood."

They followed the blood trail back to the market cross and found the square still as empty as it had been when the dragon first brought Will back. Now it was full dark, and the yellow glow from Isobel's light made the shadows around the carved stone cross and the church door opposite seem even deeper. The wind had picked up; the ends of Will's hair lashed against his face and stung the cheekbone where the dragon's tongue had left its line of fire.

"The trail goes on to the church door," Isobel said. She held the sphere of light above her head with one hand and pointed with the other at a reddish brown smear on the stone steps of the church. "If your friends think an ogre will respect the right of sanctuary . . ."

"We heard what happened to the priest," said Will. "But the church is built in stone and roofed with lead; there's no place in Caermaris more defensible, except for the castle, and that's too far away."

"Knock and see if they're inside." For the first time since Will had known her, Isobel sounded uneasy, almost afraid. "Before this light brings the ogre down on us."

"Put it out, then. I can find the door without it."

Isobel spoke another word, and the yellow glow winked out.

Will didn't wait for his eyes to adjust to the dark, but strode over to the church steps and pounded on the heavy double doors with the pommel of his sword.

"Open up!" he shouted. "Open up and let us in!"

"Will?" came a muffled voice from within. "Are you here?"

"Where else would I be if I'm talking to you?" he demanded. "Seamus, is that you?"

"And who else would I be?" The sound of scraping wood came from behind the double doors, and one of the wooden panels creaked open. Seamus's face was a pale blur against the dark interior.

"We're all in here," he said as Will and Isobel slipped through the gap in the doorway. "But we're sore hurt."

Will set his shoulder against the door and pushed it shut. Then he helped Seamus lift the massive wooden bar and settle it into place. "How bad is it?"

"Sir Garth's the worst off—he was the only one standing when the ogre came at us the second time. I was pinned under my horse, and Tostig was lying in the mud with the breath knocked out of him. By the time I'd pulled myself loose and grabbed a sword, the beast had thrown Sir Garth down and was mauling him about. But then Tostig came at the ogre from behind with his ax and split the beast's skull in two clear down to his neck-bones. After that . . . we chopped the body into as many pieces as we could and came here."

To wait for the end. Seamus didn't say the words, but Will could hear them just the same.

"I've brought something with me that may be the answer to all our prayers," Will told the squire. "Isobel—can you make the light come back, so they can see?"

She murmured something again in wizards' Latin, at the same time as Seamus said in puzzled tones, "Isobel?" And then the yellow lantern-glow lit up the interior of the church.

The sight did nothing to raise Will's spirits. Empty of worshipers, its high altar bare of linen and plate, the church of Caermaris-on-Sea seemed a cold, echoing barn of a place. A single candle guttered in a holder in the sacristy. The other two men waited there: Tostig, his bright red hair obscured by bandages torn from the linen of someone's tunic; and Garth of Orwick stretched out on a makeshift pallet, his face paler than the hair of the sea-women, the cloak that swaddled him all red and sodden with blood.

Will hurried down the nave of the church to where Garth lay. Isobel's lantern-glow kept pace with him, so that he knew without looking that she followed close behind. He went down on one knee beside Garth and spoke his friend's name. Garth opened his eyes.

"You're here again," he said. "There was a cloud of colored sparks, and you weren't with us anymore."

"It was magic," Will said. "And I've brought the ogre's death back with me."

The light from Isobel's lantern-glow shifted to fall on the ogre's egg, where it lay greenish brown and leathery in the crook of Will's arm. Garth looked at the egg for a moment. Then his pain-clouded gaze traveled upward to the source of the light, and the brief look of hope on his pale features was replaced with the resignation of utter despair.

"Lord Death's consort," he said. "The woman on the white horse. She's come to guard us until he comes."

Will felt a cold shiver go through his body. "No," he said roughly. "It's Isobel of Harrowholt, and she's a friend."

But Garth had closed his eyes and turned his face away. Will rose to his feet. The others—except for Isobel—were staring at him with a mixture of confusion, respect, and fear. He held up the egg where they could see it clearly.

"The ogre's death is in here," Will said. "A wizard showed

him how to hide it that way—so nobody could kill him unless they found the egg first and broke it to release the death."

"Do it now," said Tostig. His face was bruised and swollen where the ogre had struck to knock him out of the saddle. "Break it."

"No," Isobel said. Except for the wizards' Latin, it was the first thing she'd said since the church door opened, and her voice made Will jump. "Don't. If the ogre isn't here when the shell breaks, the death inside the egg will take the nearest victim it can find."

"Then we have to let him come in before we break it," Tostig said. He gave a short laugh. "Not so different from what we were already planning to do, is it?"

"What if the creature decides to sit on the doorstep and let us starve?" Seamus cut in. "Ogres don't have to eat their meat fresh; he'd be just as happy to see us turn into carrion all on our own."

"I don't think so," Will said. He remembered the hate that had burned in the ogre's yellow eyes. "This one, at least, holds grudges. If he knows I'm back, he'll want to kill me."

"And he doesn't know about the egg," finished Tostig. "Better shove the benches against the doors anyway, and make the beast tire himself out breaking in before we fight him. Even a mortal ogre doesn't die easily."

Will laid the egg on the high altar—he felt a pang of guilt for so despoiling a holy place, but he feared that if he put the egg anywhere else it might get lost, or broken too soon. Then he went to help Tostig and Seamus make a barricade out of the wooden benches. When they were done, he headed back toward the other end of the church, where he saw that Isobel had also been busy. She had extinguished the lantern-glow, and was using the sacristy candle to light all the other candles that stood on the altar and about the nave of the church.

"The magic light was better," Will said. "Brighter, and no moving shadows."

She looked at him soberly. "Yes. But the candles will burn whether I'm here to keep them going or not."

Will understood what she meant. She had no weapons, or any skill in their use, and no ogre could be harmed by magic.

"When the fighting starts," he said, "keep behind us."

As he spoke, a gust of wind loud enough to be heard inside the church sent rain lashing against the lead roof. For a split second the stained-glass windows dazzled with a blaze of jewelled light, and a crack of thunder made the stone foundation shake.

In the same moment the church doors cracked with a powerful blow driven from the outside.

"He's here," Isobel said. "It starts now."

The doors bent again under a crashing blow. Seamus and Tostig ran to join Will near the altar.

"Isobel, get back!" Will exclaimed.

A third time the unseen weight crashed against the doors. The heavy beam laid across them jumped and thudded in its cast-iron brackets; the oaken panels cracked and splintered.

And outside in the market square sounded the note of a hunting horn.

chapter 19

The horn sounded again, its voice torn and carried away by the sound of rain and rising wind.

Garth stirred on his pallet and lifted his head. "Lord Death has come for us, and we are lost."

Will turned to Seamus and Tostig. "Stand here by me," he said. "The doors will hold for a while yet, but they'll break before morning."

Lightning struck again, so close that the whole church was flooded with gory light driven through the scarlet-and-purple rose window above the choir. Thunder crashed like kettledrums, and hailstones rattled against the lead of the roof. Above the nave on the south side, the high, narrow window that showed the Temptation in the Desert broke inward with a crash.

Shards of colored glass and fragments of lead fell onto the stone floor, and the darkness framed by the empty window solidified and leapt down after them.

"Look out!" shouted Tostig.

The ogre came up from the floor as if the jump had been nothing. In the light of the beeswax candles, the creature looked even more fearsome and unholy than it had in the mud-paved alley. Darkness and filth were its proper habitat. Here in this place it was more than frightening; it was obscene.

"Die, you *thing*!" Seamus grabbed one of the empty candlesticks, an ell or more of solid, twisted brass, and threw it at the ogre. The ogre batted the candlestick aside with a taloned fist and laughed.

"I've come for all of you," the ogre said—*or am I the only one,* Will thought, *who can hear that howling laughter form into words?*—"and, little knights, I'll suck the marrow from your bones while you still live."

Will leapt up to the high altar and lifted his sword above the mottled, leathery egg.

"I have your death, ogre. The sea-women betrayed you."

The ogre laughed again. "Strike your blow, manling, and we'll see who's been betrayed."

Will brought his sword down against the egg. The sword rebounded in his hands, and the egg quivered under the force of the smash, but the shell didn't break. The ogre charged. Will swept his sword up and around in a full circle and a half, taking the ogre from the left side and cutting its arm in two at the elbow.

The ogre rolled away. It snatched up the severed limb with its right hand and jammed the cut end against the bleeding stump. The flesh came together and became one with no sign of any cut or scar.

"Each time you kill me, I grow stronger and heal faster," the ogre said. "The sea-women didn't tell you enough."

Will didn't bother to answer but drove in on the ogre with another attack, stepping into the blow as his sword came around. The stroke took the ogre in the abdomen, below the ribs, and should have gutted the creature—but the flesh closed like water as soon as the blade passed through it.

A figure in brown homespun darted forward: Isobel, with a thick beeswax candle grasped in both hands like a club.

She's gone mad, Will thought, before he saw how the candle burned with a torch's high, flaring light. *No. She's done some-thing to the candle. It's burning too hot for that fire to be natural.*

The long streamer of flame was bright blue at its core and glowed with the intense heat of a forge or a potter's kiln. Iso-bel swung it like a whip across the ogre's fur-covered back. The thick, oily pelt blazed up in the track of the fiery brand, filling the air with smoke and the stink of burning hair.

The ogre's entire body was covered with writhing streaks of sulfurous blue flame, but the flesh beneath them did not burn. The creature hooted derisively at Will, then rolled away under a bench as Will brought his sword down again.

The blade missed the ogre and sank into the wood of the bench. Will bit off a curse and braced his foot against the bench to pull out the blade. Before he could jerk it free a clawed hand smashed into his ribs and threw him across the bench onto the floor.

He landed hard on his back and wondered for a moment if he had broken his spine; the pain was so intense that he saw a blaz-ing light before his eyes. Then he realized that the light wasn't inside his skull. The church itself was in flames.

The blue-hot, unnatural fire from the blazing candle had touched the wooden furnishings, setting them ablaze and climb-ing the walls to reach the wooden roof that underlay the lead sheathing. The red flames were spreading from rafter to rafter over their heads.

As if we needed more trouble, Will thought.

He rolled painfully to his feet in time to see the ogre, its body outlined in a corona of blue fire, mounting the steps to the high altar and reaching for the egg. Tostig and Seamus rushed in with ax and sword to stop the creature, but it only laughed and knocked their weapons aside. Will pulled his dagger from his belt and threw himself forward into a long, low dive that caught the ogre behind its massive knees.

Will and the beast hit the floor together. The blue fire burned Will wherever it touched his bare flesh, but it was nothing compared to the searing taste of a dragon's blood, and he didn't let go his grip on the ogre. They rolled, grappling, across the stone. The ogre was heavier and stronger; it came up on top, snarling and showing a mouth lined with pointed yellow teeth. Its breath stank of carrion.

"I'll rip your face off, little man, and eat your brains."

"Eat this first!"

Will stabbed his dagger upward into the ogre's mouth as far as he could, until the point grated against bone. With its mouth wedged open, the ogre couldn't bite. It roared in frustration and tried to yank out the blade.

Will rolled away and pulled his sword from the bench. A droplet of hot metal splashed onto the flagstones beside him as the blade came free. The fire had spread even farther in the short time he and the ogre had struggled hand to hand, and a slow rain of melted lead was falling from the roof into the church below.

Outside in the market, Death's horn-call sounded again.

Will shuddered, recalling the words of the old woman under the lake: "He seeks to destroy you before you can destroy the ogre who does his bidding." Then understanding struck him with a force like the lightning that raged overhead: *She was lying when she said that! She answered three questions, and lied once—and that one was the lie!*

"The egg!" he shouted at Tostig and Seamus. "Somebody throw me the egg!"

Both squires lunged for the altar. The ogre, with Will's dagger still wedged inside its gaping mouth, grabbed them one in each hand and threw them aside—too late. Isobel, unnoticed, had already seized the egg and thrown it past the ogre into Will's outstretched hand.

Will tucked the egg under one arm and ran for the door. The pile of benches he and the others had struggled to get in place was still there, only now, instead of making entry into the church more difficult, it would make leaving almost impossible. Will dropped his sword and began tugging and shoving at the rude barricade, trying to heave the benches aside before the ogre overtook him.

He didn't dare look back over his shoulder. Even the heartbeat of time a glance would take might make the difference between success and failure. His whole body ran with sweat from the hard work of fighting and moving the benches and from the ovenlike heat of the blazing rafters overhead. The hot blue fire that wreathed the ogre's body had raised blisters on his skin wherever the creature had touched him.

He shoved the last bench away and began struggling to lift the bar one-handed without dropping the egg. Clawed fingers sank into his shoulders from behind, pulling him away—and then Tostig was there with his ax, hacking at the ogre's arms as if they were tent cables, while Seamus and Isobel heaved the bar out of its brackets and pulled open the doors.

Will pulled himself free of the ogre's grasp and staggered out onto the church steps, into the dark and the driving rain. Isobel ran after him, while behind them in the doorway Seamus and Tostig fought with sword and ax to keep the ogre from following. Lightning blazed white-purple across the wind-racked clouds overhead, so close that for an instant Will was blinded.

When his vision cleared, he saw what he had fought his way out of the burning church to see: Lord Death on his great black horse, with his troop of dead knights around him, some still with the faces they had worn in life, but pale and staring-eyed, and some only ragged scarecrows of sinew and bone. Closest of all to their lord on his black horse rode Beorn and Ohtere, with the burning church reflected in their eyes.

"Take back your own!" Will shouted at Death, and hurled the egg across the market square with all his might—just as the ogre thrust Seamus and Tostig aside and burst out of the church, burning from head to foot with blue fire and yet not consumed.

Death caught the egg and raised it over his head in one gauntleted hand.

"What is mine, I give back to the world!" he cried out in a voice of thunder, and dashed the egg to the ground.

The mottled, leathery egg broke against the cobblestones like a puffball mushroom. A black fog rose from the fragments and spread out over the market square, filling Will's nose and throat with the odor of mold and corruption. The ogre howled defiance at Death and the riders, then jerked Will's dagger out of its gaping jaws and threw the blade away into the darkness.

"You haven't killed me yet," the creature snarled at Will. "You're the one who has to do it, little knight, not your friends from the church or that one over there on his big horse. I beat him once already; I'll do it again. And all your weapons are gone."

Will's sword lay just out of reach inside the church door, where he'd dropped it to move the barricade away. He tried to dodge past the ogre and grab the blade, but the beast was too fast for him. It moved to block the way and reached for him with its long, clawed fingers.

Will flung himself out of the way at the last minute. "A sword!" he shouted as Seamus and Tostig once again moved in to bar the ogre's path. "For the love of God, somebody throw me a sword!"

Whether he cried out to his friends, or to the troop of phantoms that filled the market square, he didn't fully know. But it was Beorn of Stanburh who rode forward, spear in hand, to answer his call.

"Take my spear, Will Odosson," called Beorn. "You beat me fairly at Strickland, and I owe you my ransom still."

The ghost made as if to throw the spear to Will, but another of the pale riders spurred his horse to block the way.

"Let him die!" cried Ohtere. "Let him die and be damned—he sent me here, and I'll see him riding by my side!"

"Not while I remain in his debt," said Beorn. He couched his lance and rode at Ohtere. "Out of my way!"

Spear met shield with an impact that made no sound but filled all the square with a blaze like blue-white lightning. When the glare faded, Ohtere lay thrown from his horse on the cobblestones. Beorn of Stanburh, spear in hand, reared up over the fallen knight on his ghostly charger and threw the spear into Will's outstretched hands.

Will caught the spear in midair—but his fingers passed through the ashwood shaft as if it were made of air. The spear fell to the ground and began to drift away like mist. Then Will was aware of Isobel at his side, calling aloud in wizards' Latin as she dashed the Earl of Strickland's ivory bauble down against the cobblestones. The bauble shattered, bathing the spear in many-colored light that somehow gave the weapon's wooden shaft and iron point a solidity they had lacked before.

The ogre, roaring, shrugged off Tostig and Seamus and threw them aside. Again the creature advanced toward Will. The hovering black fog that had issued from the broken egg drew itself together and moved closer, like a blot of deeper darkness against the night. The many-colored light around the spear began to fade.

"Quickly, Will!" cried Isobel. "While the magic lasts!"

Then the ogre was upon him, and he snatched up the spear and thrust it with all the strength of his arms and shoulders into the ogre's chest, just under the arch of the ribs. The metal point slid deep into the creature's flesh.

Jagged tongues and forks of lightning split the sky above the market square. Thunder reverberated until the stone shook underfoot. The ogre howled and shrieked with defiant laughter, taking the spear in its belly and pushing forward.

The black mist swirled closer. It descended on Will, cold as a wind out of the grave, surrounding him and chilling him, running down along his arms like living smoke, but he didn't stop. He braced his feet and pushed back. The ogre was forced to give ground. Step by step Will pushed the ogre backward into the blazing church until he had the creature backed up against the carved wooden roodscreen. Then he leaned into the shaft of the spear with his full weight and drove the point deep into the wood behind the ogre's back.

The black mist poured through Will and ran along the shaft of the spear to form a pulsing halo around the ogre. The ogre screamed. The halo shrank and tightened, merging into the ogre's shape like a second skin, and sank inward until it became one with the beast.

Will left the ogre pinned there, shrieking obscenities and maledictions, and ran to where Garth lay with closed eyes on his pallet in the sacristy. He gathered up his wounded friend in his arms and half dragged, half carried him out of the burning church and into the market square where Seamus and Tostig and Isobel were waiting. They stood there amid the ranks of the dead and watched the church burn, until at last the roof collapsed in a roar and a column of ascending sparks, and the howls of the ogre ceased altogether.

"You have played your part, sir knight," Death said. "Would you know when we two shall meet again? For it is in my power to tell you."

"I don't want to know," Will said. "I didn't like knowing before."

"As you will," said Death. "But you and I ride close together,

Will Odosson; the ogre will not be the last to look on you and see my face. Farewell."

Lord Death gestured again with his hand, and his cavalcade of spectral knights followed him as he rode from the square. Last of all the knights rode Garth of Orwick, and Will knew then that his friend was dead.

The riders vanished into the darkness. The hunting horn blew again and again among the hills, growing fainter and farther away with each call until Will could hear it no more.

chapter 20

In the morning, when the storm had passed, a strong band of Nordanglian knights sent by the king at Orwick rode into Caermaris and found Will and his companions waiting there.

"We've come to deal with the ogre," said the king's champion, a big, fair-haired man in heavy armor. His shield and banner carried the king's device above his own, to show that when he acted, he acted in the king's name.

Will pointed at the church, now only a roofless pile of cracked stone and ashes steaming in the morning air. A steady rain had fallen all night, and a throat-clogging smell of wet charcoal rose from the blackened stones.

"The ogre's in there."

The king's champion looked at the ruin. "Dead?"

"Yes," said Will. "But I'd have the miller grind its bones, just the same, and throw the dust into the water at high tide. It was . . . hard to kill."

The king's champion looked down from his horse at Will and the two squires—their bodies and clothing black with smoke and smeared all about with blood and filth—and then at where Garth of Orwick lay dead at the foot of the market cross.

"I see what you mean," he said. "Your friend's past help, God rest him, but we have a healer with us who can take care of the rest of you."

The healer, a long-faced older man in a wizard's robe shortened to midcalf for riding, dismounted and came forward at the champion's gesture to look over Will and his friends. Isobel of Harrowholt was not among them. Sometime between the first sight of the approaching troop and the time the band of armed knights rode into the market square, Baron Henry's daughter had slipped away without saying good-bye. Will felt disappointed that she was gone, but also relieved. She would have been hard to explain to the king's champion—whose first thought would have been to send her home to her father's castle, to avoid problems later with Duke Anlac and the Suthanglians.

Will submitted without complaint to the healer's attentions, while some of the king's knights poked around in the ruins of the church and came out with a basket of burnt fragments that were the ogre's bones. Other knights took Garth of Orwick's body away to the churchyard and began digging a grave. The king's champion watched over everything; then, after the healer had finished with Will and gone on to Tostig, he came over and took Will aside.

"You did well," he said quietly. "The king's household always has room for brave knights, if you need a place."

Will thought a moment, then glanced over at Seamus and Tostig. "What about my friends? They've risked much for my sake, and it took all of us to bring the ogre down."

"If any squires ever earned knighthood," said the king's champion, "your companions surely did. If you want, I'll give them the accolade in the king's name before we set out for Orwick."

"It would please me greatly," said Will.

"Then it shall be done."

The king's champion bowed politely and went away again, this time to supervise the grinding up of the ogre's bones, and Will was left with nothing to do but listen to the healer muttering over Tostig's bandages. He sat for a while at the foot of the market cross, thinking of one thing and another, then stood up and wandered moodily down to the harbor.

Isobel of Harrowholt was sitting at the foot of the wooden pier, dangling her legs over the water. Will sat down next to her.

"The king's men will be coming here soon," he said, "to throw the ogre's bones into the ocean."

"I'll be gone by then," she said.

"To your teacher?"

She nodded. "She's very old and needs someone to take her place someday, to look after things in Anglia. She sees trouble ahead when the Old King dies—too many heirs, she says, on both sides of the border, and too much greed. That's why she went looking for you."

"I thought she wanted me to kill the ogre."

"She wanted to find a hero," Isobel said. "The ogre was only a start. Wizards need heroes to do the things that magic can't help with."

"Like killing things," said Will. "And watching friends die. And dying. You were Death's consort, the first time I saw him—I should have understood even then that he and I were one."

"The ogre was a wrongness in the land," Isobel said gently. "As long as it could not die, more and more death spread out from it, like filth seeping into clean water. What you did was necessary. When you killed the ogre, you brought the land back into balance."

Will gave a bitter laugh. "If your teacher plans to keep on using me for a weighing beam," he said, "she isn't likely to have me for long. I'm already prophesied to an early grave."

"No," said Isobel. "She doesn't make that kind of mistake.

Can you remember what—exactly—your father's wizard told you when he made the prophecy?"

"How could I forget it?" Will said. He closed his eyes for a moment and then spoke the words as he remembered Master Finn speaking them. "'You can take up the sword and be Sir William Odosson all your life long—but you'll meet death before any other title comes to you.'"

"That was all?"

"That was enough!"

Isobel laughed under her breath. "Then you're safe already, or at least as safe as a hero ever is. You'll never be the Baron of Restonbury now—Duke Anlac and my father between them saw to that. And as for Death, you spoke with him face-to-face last night in the market square."

"Oh." Will was silent for a moment, feeling rather stupid not to have thought of that answer himself. *So I'm not fated to die too soon after all . . . only to be cast out of my native land and have my family think I'm dead in disgrace.* His mouth twitched in what should have been a smile. "I see that outlawry and exile have advantages I hadn't thought of."

"Freedom, for one," said Isobel. "Having no oaths to bind you means that you can choose your own path and answer to no man. Some people would envy you."

Will shook his head. "A knight-errant is only one step away from a common lawbreaker at the best of times. A—a wrongness, like you say the ogre was. Something that should be bound, and isn't."

"Then find a lord who suits you better and swear to him."

Will thought of the offer the king's champion had made. "There is that," he said.

"And don't forget my teacher. When she has need of you again, she'll remember you."

Isobel stood up. There was a small sailboat tied up at the foot of the pier—it hadn't been there when Will came down to join her, though he didn't remember seeing it arrive.

"It's time for me to go," she said. "Take care, Will Odosson."

"And you," he said. "Will I see you again someday?"

"If my teacher needs you."

"You said 'when,' before."

She smiled. "You're getting the trick of listening to wizards. Until then."

"Until then," he said. He helped her down into the small boat with formal care and then cast off the line that held the boat to the pier. "Good-bye."

"Good-bye."

The boat slid away, moving through the water without the help of the wind, leaving an arrow-straight wake behind. Will stood at the end of the pier and watched its triangle of white sail grow smaller and smaller, until it was only a dot on the horizon to the west, and then nothing at all.

The harbor was empty now, and the freedom Isobel had spoken of lay on him like an unfamiliar burden. Foreknowledge, when he had it, had been easier. He remembered Master Finn's words on the eve of his knighting: *You still have a life to live in the world. Can you tell me what sort of life it will be?*

"No," he answered aloud. "No one can. But I can do my best with what comes to me."

He turned away from the sea and headed back toward the market cross, to find the king's champion and swear his oath of fealty to the king in Orwick.

about the authors

The team of DEBRA DOYLE and JAMES D. MACDONALD are the authors of many popular novels of sci-fi and fantasy, including the bestselling Mageworlds science-fantasy adventure series. Debra Doyle died in 2020. James D. Macdonald lives in New Hampshire.